THE DOOR

Georges Simenon

THE DOOR

Translated from the French by
Daphne Woodward

A Helen and Kurt Wolff Book
Harcourt Brace Jovanovich, Publishers
San Diego   New York   London

HBJ

Copyright © 1962 by Georges Simenon
English translation copyright © 1964 by Hamish Hamilton Ltd

All rights reserved. No part of this publication
may be reproduced or transmitted in any form or by any means,
electronic or mechanical, including photocopy, recording,
or any information storage and retrieval system,
without permission in writing from the publisher.

Requests for permission to make copies of any
part of the work should be mailed to:
Permissions Department,
Harcourt Brace Jovanovich, Publishers,
Orlando, Florida 32887.

This is a translation of *La Porte*,
which was first published in France in 1962.

Library of Congress Cataloging-in-Publication Data
Simenon, Georges, 1903–1989
[Porte. English]
The door/Georges Simenon;
translated by Daphne Woodward.—1st ed.
p. cm.
Translation of: La porte.
"A Helen and Kurt Wolff book."
ISBN 0-15-126370-1
I. Title.
PQ2637.I53P6613 1990
843'.912—dc20   89-19956

Designed by Kaelin Chappell
Printed in the United States of America

THE DOOR

Chapter One

THE APARTMENT BUILDING, like many other old ones in this part of Paris, had tall, narrow windows that came down to within twelve inches of the floor and were traversed by a cast-iron railing whose arabesques supported a wooden bar. It was through these arabesques that Bernard Foy, from his chair, kept a rather absentminded eye on the comings and goings in the street below. He frowned on seeing Dr. Aubonne's little blue car come around the corner from rue des Francs-Bourgeois into rue de Turenne, cross the street at an oblique angle, and pull up behind the truck belonging to Herbiveaux's, the stationery shop.

The doctor put his head out the window to make sure he was not too far from the curb, reversed, gave a little jerk forward, came to a final stop, and squeezed his way out of the tiny car.

Bernard was uncertain about the date. He never knew it precisely. July 5 or 6; at latest the 7th. Another week and they would be kept awake all night by the brass bands and fireworks of the July 14 celebrations in Place des Vosges.

School was not closed for the summer yet. Half an hour ago, children had come rushing out with shrill screams, to scamper homeward in all directions.

Although he did not know the date, he knew it must be Monday, because yesterday Nelly and he had sat with the windows wide open, and the street had been so quiet and empty they might have thought themselves alone in Paris. At one time, about noon, there had been no living creature in sight except a dog roaming aimlessly along the deserted sidewalk.

In any case, the doctor was early. He generally came to rue de Turenne in the late afternoon of the day in the third week of each month when he called on the crippled old woman who lived on rue de Sévigné.

What made Bernard wonder all of a sudden whether that story was true, whether that old woman really existed? Dr. Aubonne refused to let him pay for these monthly visits, on the pretext that he came more as a friend than as a doctor—which seemed plausible enough, after a twenty-year acquaintance.

Usually, after reversing his car rather clumsily, with his head out the window, he glanced up at the fifth floor, knowing he would see Bernard Foy sitting at a window as surely as, from one year's end to the next, a canary could be seen in its cage in an opposite window, above the stationery shop.

Aubonne would then make a gesture, as though, passing by chance, to ask, "May I come up?"

Why shouldn't he come up? He was never in the way. He knew that at this time of day, and at most others,

Bernard was alone with his lampshades and paintbrushes. The gesture was a tradition, a way of making his visit seem friendly but unpremeditated.

Yet he always brought his rusty old bag, which had not been new even when the two men first met, at the beginning of the war.

But today the doctor did not look up. Why did he act as though unaware that Bernard was watching him? And why was he at least a week ahead of schedule?

Had Nelly called him up and asked him to come sooner? And, knowing he must not give her away, he was feeling awkward at having to tell a lie and put on an act?

Two men in blue coveralls were lifting heavy flat boxes out of the truck, the side of which had the name in bold yellow letters: WIDOW HERBIVEAUX / WHOLESALE STATIONER. Madame Herbiveaux did a retail trade as well; the schoolchildren bought their supplies at her double-fronted shop.

The doctor made two attempts to close the door of the car; the second time he banged it too hard. Then he set off across the street, bag in hand, wagging his head as though it were overburdened with thoughts, and paying no attention to the traffic.

What was he thinking about? What, in fact, did he think of Bernard Foy and his wife and the life they had been leading together for the last twenty years in their apartment on rue de Turenne, above Escandon's pastry shop at the corner of rue des Minimes?

He knew Bernard better, no doubt, than anyone else—from both the medical and the human point of view—after watching him so often with those bulging eyes, which gave him a shrewd yet ingenuous expression. Did he really know him, though?

He stopped by only once a month, though it had been more often in the old days; he had other patients, more interesting cases, at Saint-Antoine Hospital and in his private practice. He performed as many as five operations a day, had a wide circle of colleagues and friends, played bridge now and then. Besides all that, there was his family: a wife he had loved at one time and perhaps still did, and three sons, two of whom were married.

How could Bernard occupy more than a small corner of his world and his attention? The doctor was a faithful friend, of course. After all this time he kept up his visits as though they were still necessary. Did he ever wonder about Bernard? Or did he assume that all his problems were solved?

It was a sweltering day. The sun had not yet sunk behind the roofs across the street; it was casting long, shiny rectangles on the polished floor.

But because the room had two windows overlooking rue de Turenne and one on rue des Minimes, there was an intermittent draft, which felt like cold water trickling over the skin.

Bernard, without quite knowing why, felt uncomfortable, uneasy. He was mentally following the doctor, who was now in the building, having gone past the concierge's lodge and no doubt touched the brim of his gray hat, which he wore all year round.

There was no elevator. The stairs were worn, but carefully polished. At each bend, on the landing, there was a darker stretch, and the doctor always paused there to catch his breath.

When Bernard had seen him the first time, in uniform, looking like a civilian disguised as an officer, his fat legs enclosed in brown leather puttees, he had been a man of forty-four or forty-five, with hair that was beginning to recede, making his big head look even bigger.

So now he must be sixty-five. He had heart trouble and diabetes, and once, when Nelly was there, he had asked if he might go into the bathroom to give himself an insulin injection.

Bernard was still following Aubonne's progress upstairs, guessing at the sounds he would be hearing from beyond the different doors as he went: the typewriter on the second floor, where Monsieur Jussieu, translator for the law courts, lived, the piano on the third floor, where Mademoiselle Strieb gave lessons to little girls; perhaps Mademoiselle Renée's record player or radio on the fourth floor, or old Madame Meilhan's voice in the opposite apartment, trying to make herself heard by her deaf husband.

Bernard thought the climb was taking longer than usual, and, for no definite reason, sweat broke out on his forehead. He got up before the doctor had reached his own floor, and went across to the door, forcing a smile.

It was ridiculous, he knew, feeling a little ashamed of his reaction. Perhaps everything about him had been ridiculous recently. If so, that made it even worse.

He stood facing the closed door, motionless, with a tightness across his chest, listening to the doctor's footsteps on the last stairs and his heavy breathing as he waited outside to catch his breath before knocking. He could imagine Aubonne's movements, the handkerchief with which he was mopping his forehead and his stubbly cheeks, the cigarette he was relighting because it went out whenever he had to climb stairs.

Aubonne knocked, and Bernard, to make things seem normal, walked around for a few steps before opening the door.

"I was afraid you wouldn't be home. . . ."

The doctor had a frank, open face. In the last few years he had put on weight because of the diabetes. He was wearing his invariable navy-blue suit, the cloth of which was getting rather shiny, and his tie was crooked, as usual.

"I haven't been out for so long now. . . ."

"You should! You should!"

His eyes traveled around the big room, which he knew well; it was both dining room and living room—and studio, too, because it was there that Bernard painted his lampshades. There were three of them on the table now; he always did three at a time, putting on all the red, then all the blue or the mauve or the green. For several weeks he had been repeating the same pattern, a design that had been supplied to him—roses alternating with iris. Why iris? He neither knew nor cared.

"I came today—and will see my old paralyzed patient as well—because on Saturday I have to be in Lisbon for a congress. My wife's going with me, and we'll take a week or two of vacation in Portugal while we're at it."

He didn't behave like a sick man, though he must be more aware of his condition than anyone else. He went on talking about the trip with almost childish delight as he put down his bag and settled into his usual chair, Nelly's.

"And how are you, my friend?" he asked.

"All right, thank you."

"Hard at work, as usual?" continued the doctor, pointing to the lampshades and the little pots of paint.

"I can't sit doing nothing all day. Besides, it wouldn't be fair to my wife."

He tried to guess from Aubonne's reaction whether Nelly had telephoned him.

"How is she?"

"Fine. Younger than ever."

6

He could not stop himself from saying that, though it sprang from nothing except, perhaps, his secret worries. In fact, Nelly was not much younger than he was. When they married, she had been eighteen and he twenty-two. Now she was thirty-eight.

Had Aubonne been struck by this reference to Nelly's age? Had he already guessed Bernard's concealed anxiety, or had Nelly given him a hint when she called him?

He said in a tone of deep conviction, "She's a wonderful woman."

"Yes, she's amazing," agreed Bernard, with a faint suggestion of bitterness.

"Won't you be going away together this summer?"

"Her vacation begins next month, but we'll stay in Paris."

"Why?"

Bernard looked away.

"What's the use?" he muttered.

"You still have attacks of dizziness?"

"Yes."

"Several times a day?"

"Yes."

"When does it happen, mostly?"

"Anytime. Sometimes as soon as I get up. Other times, when I sit down at the table, or simply when I move from one chair to another."

He had already told the doctor this, not once but a dozen times at least, and he was beginning to wonder whether people believed him, or whether they thought he was pretending.

Why should he pretend, for heaven's sake? The doctor didn't pretend to be a diabetic, did he? And his two heart attacks—he hadn't faked them, had he?

Bernard was fond of Aubonne. Next to Nelly, the doctor

7

was his closest human contact, the only person with whom he had felt at ease for twenty years.

But today he was annoyed with him, and felt he ought to apologize for the feeling.

"According to Pellet, they should gradually have gone away."

A few months ago, when Bernard first complained of dizziness, Aubonne had sent him to see a specialist, Pellet. The two men could not have been more different. Pellet was a big shot, and never forgot it. Bernard had gone to his clinic for a consultation and found him surrounded by a group of four or five assistants, who listened to the man with awe; and it was for their benefit that he talked and asked questions.

"Let's see . . . You were wounded in 1940 by a grenade, which took off both your hands."

"Not a grenade; a mine. We were patrolling a wood between the Maginot and Siegfried lines. I was crawling in the snow and I must have touched a mine. It exploded. . . ."

"You were wounded in the head?"

"No. Only the hands. When I came to, in the local château—which had been turned into a hospital—I found my hands gone, and . . ."

The specialist was not listening. Unlike Aubonne, he wanted short, definite replies; the rest did not interest him. He broke in curtly: "Who was the first doctor who attended you? Do you know?"

"Dr. Aubonne."

"You had lost both hands, but you had no other injuries, is that right?"

"Yes."

"And since then you have never felt any pain in your head?"

"Not until the last few months."

"What kind of pain is it, exactly?"

The specialist took notes as though doodling during someone else's speech. He was tall and thin and had protruding teeth, which made him look aggressive even when he smiled.

"In the street . . ."

"You were in the street when you felt the first symptoms?"

"Yes—I think so. I was crossing. There was a lot of noise, because of the traffic and because some workmen were drilling a hole. For some time before . . ."

He was struggling to be objective, fumbling for the right words. During the war, after he was wounded, he had been moved from one hospital to another, and each time he had been surrounded and questioned by men in white. But none of them had intimidated him as much as this Pellet.

"I felt as though my head was spinning, the way it does when you get off a merry-go-round. . . . I felt sure I'd be run over."

The doctor glanced complacently at his assistants and then repeated, stressing each word separately. "The way it does when you get off a merry-go-round, you say?"

"Yes."

"Your head was spinning?"

"Yes."

"And you felt sick, a kind of seasick feeling?"

"I've never been on the sea."

"You felt like vomiting?"

"No."

The specialist's eyes became wary, as though he suspected Bernard of trying to deceive him.

"You have not been hearing well, lately?"

"Oh, no. My ears have been getting more sensitive. Certain sounds, especially high-pitched ones, literally hurt, like an instrument piercing my eardrums. It makes me depressed and irritable."

The specialist was not interested in his patient's moods. That was the first consultation. There had been two others. He had been subjected to a series of rather unpleasant tests, such as pouring ice water into his ears and making him spin around and around. He had been X-rayed. He had been asked questions—the same and others—with greater persistence, as though in the hope that he would contradict himself.

Most of all, they wanted to know whether he was certain he had not been wounded in the head. The X ray, it seemed, showed what Pellet called "a microscopic fracture of the petrosal bone."

"Ask Dr. Aubonne. He's the one who knows. At that time, I wasn't capable of judging what state I was in."

The specialist was exasperated when the facts refused to conform to his theories, especially since he had written several books on the subject.

In the end, he had prescribed tranquilizers.

"Do you sleep well?"

"I used to."

"Until when?"

"Until just lately."

"And now you suffer from insomnia?"

"I lie awake every night for most of two hours before getting to sleep."

"Do you feel annoyed?"

"No. I just wait."

"You have no worries?"

"None at all."

"There have been no new developments in your life?"

"No."

"You go out, in spite of your dizzy spells?"

"As little as possible."

"Are you afraid of falling down in the street? Do you feel as though you're likely to fall?"

"I don't think so. But I don't feel safe, especially when there's a lot of activity and noise. In the evening, when the streets are almost deserted, my wife and I go to Place des Vosges and walk around it two or three times."

"And the giddiness doesn't bother you?"

"Oh, yes. I sometimes have to stand still for a moment. . . ."

"Because things begin to turn around and around?"

"Yes . . . No—it's not that, exactly. I feel shaky. I feel insecure, a kind of panic; my knees begin to wobble, and sweat breaks out on my forehead. . . ."

Did they or did they not believe him? Not just Pellet and his assistants—among whom was a very beautiful woman—but Aubonne, to whom the specialist had sent a written report.

Right now, Aubonne was still looking at him with his big eyes, as though trying to find the truth. His questions were less direct, less personal.

"According to Pellet . . ."

Bernard felt like shouting at him: "I'm not ill in order to contradict Dr. Pellet! It's not my fault if what's happening inside me isn't what he describes in his books. I know more about my own feelings than he does, don't I?"

"I wonder if it wouldn't be a good thing for you and your wife to have two or three weeks in the country or at the seaside. Do you like the sea?"

He, too, spoke as though the sea were just down the street.

"I've never seen it."

Nor had Nelly, for that matter. When he was a child, his family had been too poor to go to the sea for a vacation. It had been the same for her. Then, he had done his army national service at Epinal, in the opposite direction from the sea, and that was where he had met Nelly.

Afterward, as soon as they were married, they had come to live here, only a step from Place des Vosges, where he had been born and where at that time his mother was still concierge.

That was early in 1939. A few months later, war came, and he had been called up. In February, when nothing was happening except patrols that were more like peacetime maneuvers, he had had both hands blown off by a mine.

So when could he have gone to the seaside? Not while they were handing him on from one hospital or rehabilitation center to the next! And since then, with the two hooks, which he had at last grown accustomed to, he had never felt really at ease except in his own apartment. Particularly nowadays, when he kept having these bouts of dizziness.

"You know, Bernard, you've always been so brave, but I'm wondering whether your courage hasn't given way a little these last few weeks."

And Bernard wondered whether the doctor had thought of this himself, or whether Nelly had prompted him. She would never dare make such a suggestion herself. She never mentioned his health, but kept up her usual blithe spirits. Still, he felt sure she was worried.

Worried about what, exactly? That was the thing he wanted to know, and was trying to guess behind Aubonne's words.

"For your wife, too, a real holiday, in some very quiet place . . ."

"You've seen her?"

"Not since the last time I met her here."

The doctor's blue eyes were unclouded. It was Bernard who felt awkward, ashamed, annoyed with himself. If he was mistaken, his attitude was quite contemptible. And he was just as likely to be wrong as right—even more so.

"It's only here that I feel comfortable."

"I understand. But you ought to stir yourself. You've got into an unhealthy situation, and that's not good for anybody. How long has it been since you last went out?"

"Two weeks ago we went to the movies on Boulevard du Temple."

"And since then?"

"We've been two or three times to Place des Vosges for a breath of air."

How could he explain that he was finding it more and more unpleasant, even frightening, to emerge from his own little corner?

Pellet had said, almost angrily: "In fact, you're shutting yourself up."

That was not true. Never before had he taken so much interest in other people's lives, whether outdoors or in the building. He could recognize the step of every tenant and every delivery man; whenever a door opened and closed he knew who was coming in or going out.

He could almost have repeated the words of greeting that people exchanged when they met, and described their movements.

According to Pellet and the results of the tests, he was growing slightly deaf. Whereas in point of fact he had never heard sounds so acutely—to such an extent that he really suffered whenever the children got out of school and made their invariable shrill cries.

He had reached the point of waiting impatiently for the children to go away on vacation, and he almost hated the Rougin twins in the next apartment because they banged the front door, just as the doctor had banged the door of his car.

"And your hands?"

Aubonne always spoke of his "hands," knowing that for Bernard they were still there, that he could still feel pain in them.

"All right—except when it's very damp or humid. I'm used to that."

"No eczema?"

He had had a lot of it at first, before he got used to his hooks. Nowadays he was careful to keep his skin in good condition.

"How long is it since you went to see old Hélias?"

"Last month. He adjusted the prosthesis, and I'm to go again in three or four weeks."

Hélias was his orthopedist, on rue du Chemin-Vert. He had fitted Bernard with the only prostheses he could tolerate, and for the last eighteen years the old man had continued to keep it in repair, adjusting it or making an improvement every now and then.

"I'd like to take your blood pressure."

Aubonne always did that, and it was the only medical action of his visit. He opened his bag with precise, almost loving movements, like old Hélias handling his precision tools.

"Perfectly normal. I would guess your pressure falls during a dizzy spell. But to make certain, I'd need to be with you at the time. You still drink no wine or alcohol?"

"Half a glass of wine, with water, at each meal."

He had long ago been forbidden to drink, like everyone

who has lost a limb. And because of his dizziness, Pellet had advised him to give up coffee. Except for the coffee, he didn't mind. He had no temptation to drink and could still look life straight in the face.

He had never complained. He did not think of himself as a man to be pitied, but as one who had had a miraculous escape—for he should really have been blown to bits by the mine. At the field hospital, at first, they had thought he was a hopeless case, and if Aubonne had not taken an interest in him, he would probably not have pulled through.

Wasn't it another miracle to have found Nelly again? And yet another that she'd gone on living with him?

As the doctor had said, nodding his big head, she was a wonderful woman. He did his best to deserve her. For that very reason . . .

"I'm not pleased, Bernard."

"With me?"

"With seeing you like this. Last time I came, I got the impression that you were worried and weren't telling me everything. Today I don't feel I'm in touch with you at all. Tell me frankly—do these dizzy spells frighten you?"

"When you've been through what I've been through and come out of it alive, you're not easily scared."

"That's not an answer. Do you think about it?"

"Whenever a spell comes on."

"Why do you call it a spell?"

"I don't know. For lack of a better word, I guess. It's like a spell, I imagine, in the way it begins, intensifies, dies down and is over."

"I wonder . . ."

Aubonne hesitated, pausing to light a cigarette, which he would allow to go out, like the last one.

"What do you wonder?"

"I don't want to talk like Pellet. I know you don't like him or trust him. But I'm wondering if you don't, to some extent, enjoy this business, whether the trouble isn't more psychological than physical."

"The X rays . . ."

"I know. Pellet told me."

"He's determined that my symptoms should fit in with his ideas. I can't help it if . . ."

"For twenty years you've borne your disablement with courage that I admire. What I'm wondering is . . . You're forty years old now. . . ."

"Forty-two."

"That's an age when a man is inclined to take stock of his life, to look back and sum things up, as it were. . . ."

"I'm not the sort of fellow to stare into a mirror. You know that."

"And your wife?"

"What about her?"

"I suppose she's the same as usual? Last time I came, she didn't seem to have changed."

"She's more cheerful and attentive than ever."

He didn't like to see the doctor coming so dangerously near the real point. He didn't feel sure of himself, and he might easily give himself away. So he spoke with all the more conviction.

"We're a happy couple, as you've often said yourself."

"Yes . . ."

Aubonne seemed to be hesitating about whether to insist, to go further, like someone searching a wound. He stood up and sighed.

"Oh, well!"

That meant nothing, except that he was not satisfied with the conversation and felt reluctant to go.

"Anyhow, think over what I said about a vacation trip. There are still villages in France where you wouldn't be swamped in a flood of tourists."

"We're by ourselves here, too. . . ."

The apartment was cheerful and comfortable. They were used to it and found it convenient. Nobody in their district was surprised, any longer, to see a man with hooks instead of hands walking arm in arm with a pretty woman. Nobody turned to look back at them. Nobody felt sorry for him, or for her.

What would be the good of starting again somewhere else and forming new habits for just a few weeks? Was it even certain that Nelly would want to go away, now?

He almost said aloud, "I'm not sure that my wife . . ."

But then the doctor would have one end of the thread and would want to follow it. And there was nothing for him to know.

"Have a good time in Portugal."

"Oh, I'll be back in harness a fortnight from now."

Since he could not shake hands, Aubonne touched him lightly on the shoulder, as usual.

"See you next month, Bernard."

"Good-bye, doctor."

He shut the door and listened as the footsteps retreated downstairs. In the next apartment, Madame Rougin was having a fight with the twins; she began a real row, almost a battle, with them every day as soon as they got home from school. They were thirteen years old, with sandy crewcut hair and unblinking violet eyes.

The sun had crossed the frontier of the rooftops, and the chimneypots were the same shade of pink as the roses on Bernard's lampshades.

He stood for a moment, head bent, in the middle of the

room. Then he heard the door of the doctor's car slam. The truck had gone. The little blue car swerved dangerously and went off toward Place des Vosges, where children were shrieking in the central garden.

It was time to heat things for dinner. Without haste, he put away his paints and lampshades, went into the kitchen, and lit the gas under the saucepan of soup.

A little later, he would set the two places, opposite each other, on the table near the window. He still had time to spare, and he leaned on the window rail and looked down at the people going by in the street; now and then he heard the familiar tinkle of a shop-door bell.

In a few minutes Nelly would be leaving work, at Delangle & Abouet, on Place des Victoires. She would stand chatting for a moment with her friend Gisèle, who would perhaps give her a small package, and then she'd get her bus. Presently he would see her get off, nearly opposite the house, look up, and wave to him with a smile.

Maybe she would go to the pastry shop to get something for dessert.

Maybe . . . Would she stop on the second floor again today?

He lit a cigarette, and the smoke drifted slowly away in the rosy air outside.

Chapter Two

IN A WAY, their household was the reverse of other people's. It was he who waited for his wife to come home
from work. It was he who stayed at home all day, Nelly
who flitted off every morning—in winter by the cold, gray
light of dawn—and spent the greater part of her time in
an unknown world; it was she who met people Bernard
didn't know, except some, by name, and who took part in
activities in which he had no share.

He was not exactly jealous, but each time he saw her
on the other side of the street, waiting for the bus, and she
gave him a last encouraging smile, he felt a slight pang.

For a time—only a few months—it had been the other
way around; he stood in the street looking up, and carried
away a picture of Nelly in her dressing gown leaning on
the window rail.

At that time he could imagine her all day in the apartment, which had not yet seemed permanent; it looked more
like temporary quarters.

How happy it was then, their home! Thinking back over that period of their existence, he saw it as unbelievably carefree. He could remember nothing but sunny days, as though it had never rained, as though for nearly a year the sky had never been gray. His memory would admit only one heavy storm cloud; all the time it was there, he had sung at the top of his voice, to tease his wife because she was afraid, or to reassure her—trying in vain to drown the noise of the thunder with his singing.

When he got married, his mother had rallied all the other concierges in the district and found him an apartment; the old woman who had lived alone there for forty years had just died. The wallpaper in her living room—now their living room—had been thick, with a raised pattern in gold on dark brown, imitating Spanish leather, and it showed a kind of ghostly outline of the former furniture and pictures.

"We can be thankful the old woman's ghost isn't here, too!" he had said jokingly, unaware that his wife believed in ghosts.

Even after two months, the bedroom still smelled of old woman and sickness.

Bernard was then a mechanic, working at a garage near the central markets. He had asked for three days off to scrape away the wallpaper, and he had had to dab it with acid before it would come off. Underneath, they had found more and older layers, even more obstinately adhesive. They laughed while they peeled away the past history of their apartment.

"She's a sticker, the old woman!" Bernard would complain.

Under the brown paint of the floor, they found red tiles; Nelly went down on her knees and washed them clean—

first scrubbing them with a stiff-bristled brush and then, when that proved inadequate, with a wire one.

They had scarcely any savings and had been obliged to pay six months' rent in advance, including a quarter more for security, in case they were ever in arrears or did some damage.

They had no furniture at the beginning except a bed and a wardrobe they bought from a secondhand dealer on rue des Blancs-Manteaux and brought home in a handcart. On Sunday mornings they used to go to the flea market, where everything looked wonderful to them because they needed everything.

Nelly was not working then. He wouldn't let her, considering that he earned enough for them both. Besides, he needed to find her at home, watching at the window for his return.

If asked to explain how he felt about her, he might perhaps not have used the word "love," but he would have spoken of a need—he needed her presence. And during the hours he spent at the garage, he needed to know, hour by hour, where she was and what she was doing.

"Now she'll be going out, wearing her red dress, with no hat."

She had only two dresses, and the red was the cotton one she wore around the house and to do her local shopping.

"She'll be going into the greengrocer's, the one kept by Madame Pauquet, who has a southern accent and says "tu" to all her women customers. . . ."

His thoughts followed her as he lay on his back under a car or bent over his workbench, and it was nice to remind himself that he wasn't alone, that there were two of them now, that Nelly belonged to him.

21

"This is fish day. . . ."

Or pork-chop day; for they were beginning to develop habits and traditions. She often came to get him at noon-time, and they walked home together, or, occasionally, went to eat lunch at a little restaurant in the central markets.

In the evening, she waited for him a few yards from the garage, and his co-workers would tease him, pretending to believe she was keeping an eye on him. He knew that wasn't true. It was he who asked her to come, so they'd be separated as little as possible.

"Who's that tall, rough-looking man who stares at me so rudely?"

"Louis? He's the nicest fellow in the place. He's married, too. His wife's just had a baby, so she can't come to get him the way she used to until a few weeks ago—tremendously proud of her big belly, she was."

From time to time, they dropped in on his mother in Place des Vosges—on the far side, the part that belongs to the Fourth Arrondissement, not the Third. Bernard would open the glass-paneled door under the arch, and they would sit down in a stifling smell of cooking.

His sister, Olga, was not yet married, but they seldom saw her. She was three years younger than Bernard and spent most of her time running around with boyfriends.

"One of these days she'll be coming home with a baby on the way!" Madame Foy would say mournfully.

Fate is really unpredictable! Olga used to haunt the worst dance halls on rue de Lappe. Like a cat in heat, she would vanish every now and then, and it was sometimes two or three days before they heard from her.

But about halfway through the war she calmly announced that she was getting married, and it was true. She married an excellent fellow, six years older, who worked for the railway, and they bought a little house out in Juvisy.

She bore him three children in rapid succession, two girls and a boy. Now she was a plump young matron, kept her house in apple-pie order and never went out, except to the movies with her husband every Saturday.

It was she who had made a home for their mother when she grew too old for the duties of a concierge, and the old woman thought the world of her nowadays.

The past seemed unreal. For Bernard it remained more alive than for the others, as a strange, almost impossible life. He thought of it without bitterness or regret, but with a perpetual astonishment.

They had been through that, the pair of them! After twenty years they were still together, in the same apartment, where sturdy, rustic-style furniture had gradually settled into permanent positions.

He was waiting. He spent his life waiting for Nelly, and when at last she was there he hardly felt the need to talk to her. She was close to him, within the same walls, breathing the same air, and that was all he needed for contentment.

It had been like that at Epinal, too, almost as soon as they met. She was an usherette at the Palace movie house on rue Gambetta, and one day he happened to be sitting next to the tip-up seat she used to occupy stealthily while the show was on.

Whenever the screen was bright, he turned to watch her face, which he thought looked sulky and a little timid, and the way her hair flopped over it whenever she moved her head.

From time to time she went away, shining her flashlight in front of her, to seat some late arrival; and he, uninterested in the film, followed her with his eyes, hoping each time that everyone had come in at last.

He had returned several times that week, even though he had to leave before the end to be back in his barracks by ten o'clock. Not until Saturday, when he had a pass until midnight, did he pluck up courage to wait for her on the way out.

He could still see the other man, who had frightened him so much—a man who was waiting, too, vaguely seen by the lights of the Brasserie du Globe, in the same building as the movie house. He was older, well-dressed, and the motorcycle parked by the curb must be his.

There were three usherettes at the Palace. Was it credible that the man would have chosen any but his, whose name he didn't yet know?

He had, however, and the motorcycle had driven off with a small, fat, giggly blonde, just as Nelly, wearing a black dress, came out and glanced around as though expecting to find him there.

Hadn't she been smiling as she set off briskly along the sidewalk, and wasn't she listening to Bernard's footsteps behind her? When he caught up, all she said was, "Oh, it's you!"

He had escorted her to within a hundred yards of her home, which was outside town, near the firing range, and he had to run all the way back to his quarters to avoid being late.

Maybe he'd really been waiting for her ever since that evening.

Her name was Rabaud, and she lived with five brothers and sisters in a kind of hut on a piece of wasteland.

Her father was a manual laborer and was never seen without a bottle of red wine sticking out of the pocket of his corduroy jacket.

As for her mother, a fat woman with a mottled red face, who was known as La Rabaude, there were sly grins whenever her name was mentioned, even among the soldiers, when they went out to drill not far from the hut. Bernard preferred to ignore the gossip about her, which was probably exaggerated.

Every day he waited for the time when he could go to the movie house and take his seat, always the same one at the end of the back row. He waited again at the beginning of the show, between the newsreel and the documentary, when people were still arriving and Nelly was busy, her little light dancing ahead of her.

Then he waited for Sunday, to hurry to the firing range, where she would join him by ten o'clock in the morning.

For eighteen months they had taken walks, first hand in hand, later each with an arm around the other's waist, in the woods and beside the Moselle.

He could not have said what attracted him to her, and he hadn't asked her to become his mistress. It was she who, after three or four weeks, when they had been picnicking under a beech tree and were lying side by side with their fingers interlaced, had whispered to him: "Don't you want to?"

He was perhaps a little disappointed to discover in this way that she had been with other men, but it made no difference. He went on spending his free evenings at the movie house.

One day she gave him some tickets, ones that were distributed to local shopkeepers for putting posters in their windows. So he had only the entertainment tax to pay.

They never spoke of the future. They were more concerned with Monsieur Boutang, the boss—Monsieur Félix, they called him—who had become their personal enemy owing to his habit of suddenly arriving and standing motionless at the back, as though watching them.

He was a short, fat man with a head almost as big as

Dr. Aubonne's and pale, expressionless eyes. He walked with his legs wide apart and his toes turned out, and you never heard him coming. You suddenly felt that he was behind you, peering around.

He owned both the movie house and the Brasserie du Globe, into which he tried to lure the audience. Whenever Nelly sat down beside Bernard in the dark and their hands met, one of them—sometimes both together—would look around to make sure Monsieur Félix was not standing just behind them.

He used to stay at the back for quite a long time at the beginning of each program. Then he went back to the brasserie, and returned shortly before the intermission. In the course of the evening he would make several other silent, furtive appearances, and Bernard was convinced, rightly or wrongly, that they were aimed at him.

He had even asked Nelly, in his anxiety, whether Monsieur Félix had any grounds for jealousy.

"Him? He'd never dare make eyes at any of us girls. He's far too scared of his wife!"

Maybe he was jealous of them for being in love, for being young, for being so happy together in the dark, in the back row. Bernard could have sworn that was it, and this, too, had become a pleasant memory.

On Saturdays and Sundays he saw the same film twice, at the matinee and in the evening. A big hit sometimes ran for two weeks, so that in the end he knew the lines by heart. There were whole scripts he could still have reeled off from memory. Some of them came back to mind when he was alone in the apartment, working on his lampshades.

It had been a special treat for them to be able to meet in the daytime during the week; that needed long planning and much diplomacy. Fatigue parties were sent to the firing range now and then, and Bernard got himself included in these when he could or arranged to take another fellow's place.

It was like stolen time. He saw her out of doors in the sunshine and later on in the snow. For a whole winter they made love in the snow, and would laugh when Nelly got up and found snow between her thighs.

On those days, too, he waited for her, in a fever of impatience, just as she used to wait for him after they were married.

It was wonderful! How could he grumble at fate when it had given him such happiness, and still did? The most curious thing was that in those days he hadn't realized Nelly was pretty. Perhaps she hadn't been, as yet? He didn't care. He never gave it a thought. She was herself, and that was enough.

He remembered her mouth—a funny one, he used to say, because the lower lip pouted in a peculiar way that made her look sulky. Even now they sometimes talked about her hair as it had been then, when she deliberately let it get tangled and fall over her face, shaking it back now and again with a jerk of her head.

She had been thin, almost without hips or breasts, and he had taken years to notice that she had changed.

In fact, it wasn't too long ago that it had occurred to him that she was beautiful, or pretty—in any case, more desirable at thirty-eight than she had been at twenty. She no longer seemed shy and sulky, but gave the impression of a gentle, plump little woman with a merry, comforting smile.

Could she really have been happy with him all these years? Was she still? He could hardly believe it, and the doubt bothered him. For the last few months, and particularly the last few weeks, he had been tormenting himself all the time. Aubonne was right about that. But his trouble was not what the doctor imagined.

He set two places at the table, which had a red-checked cloth, like a country inn's. It was probably with such inns in mind—though they had seldom been to one—that they had furnished the apartment in a rustic manner and put copper pots and pans on the shelves.

The smell of leek soup wafted from the kitchen. He lit another cigarette and went back to lean out of the window, watching for the bus. He could see its silvery roof gliding along the deep trench of the street, like the back of some huge animal.

The bus stopped. A woman got out, but it was not Nelly. It was the vivacious brunette who lived by herself above the fish shop and was visited every Saturday by a man, always the same one.

She never shut the window or drew the curtains. The man—about forty—used to take off his jacket, tie, and shoes, put on a brown dressing gown and slippers, and sit by the window reading the newspaper, while the woman cleared the table and washed the dishes.

After that she would sit down opposite him, and they could be seen talking for a long time, motionless and with impassive faces, until nearly everyone else on the street had gone to bed. Then the woman would take off her dress and sit down at her dressing table, sometimes in her slip and sometimes with nothing on but her bra and panties.

She, too, waited for something on Saturdays, just opposite the Foys', on the same floor.

There was another woman who waited at the window every evening, for her husband—an older woman with a worn, anxious face. In the mornings she used to lean out and watch him as he went to catch a bus at the corner of rue des Francs-Bourgeois. He walked slowly and often had to make a long pause, with his hand pressed to his chest. Aubonne, to whom Bernard had spoken about it, supposed he must have heart trouble.

Nelly was not ill, and yet he was uneasy because she had not got off the bus that was now moving on. It was a strange, subtle kind of anxiety, not to be overcome by reason. He was not necessarily imagining an accident or other disaster, much less that his wife might have run away and left him.

It was a *lack*, he called it in his mind. He had found no better word. He felt the lack of Nelly's presence, and that was enough to throw him off balance. Not because he was disabled! It wasn't on account of his hooks that he needed her, since he'd had the same feeling at Epinal when he had known her for scarcely three weeks.

She would arrive by the next bus. Her friend Gisèle must have delayed her outside their office, chattering and asking her to do things for her brother.

"You hate Gisèle, don't you?" Nelly had once remarked, laughing.

He didn't hate her—he hated no one—but of all the people he knew, he resented her the most. She had started working at Delangle & Abouet five or six years ago, shortly after her marriage to a fellow named Lebesque.

Bernard knew them both; they had been up to the apartment several times. Lebesque was a flabby, fair-haired man, always impeccably dressed, and so proud of his job at the headquarters of Crédit Lyonnais, on the Grands Boulevards, that one would have thought he had charge of all the safe-deposit keys. Yet he insisted that his wife work, too, even after they had had one, then two, and now three children.

They lived in a rent-controlled apartment near Porte

d'Orléans, and both of them took it for granted that other people should be at their beck and call. For instance, it was Lebesque's aunt, a pathetic old lady with bad varicose veins, who looked after the three children from morning till night; after which she had to take the Métro right across Paris to her home on rue Lamarck.

When Gisèle's brother had had polio and been left with nowhere to live, Gisèle had said to Nelly: "You might make inquiries in your district. They say the Marais has the greatest proportion of old people, and some of them die every day; so it makes space."

The annoying thing was that she got away with it. Monsieur François, the old gentleman with private means who lived in two rooms on the second floor, behind the translator's apartment, had died that very week. He was eighty-six and had been paralyzed for so long that some of the tenants didn't even know he existed.

"You don't mind if I ask the concierge whether his apartment is free? Gisèle would be so pleased!"

Nelly always did her best to please people. Could he decently object?

"Her brother has just spent five months at a rehabilitation center, but it will be a long time, perhaps years, before he'll be able to walk properly."

"What about his sister? Couldn't she take him in?"

"Oh, come, Bernard! With three children, in an apartment that has only four rooms including the kitchen! They're too cramped as it is."

"All right, speak to the concierge."

"You don't mind?"

"No."

Perhaps he ought to have said yes; his wife would not have insisted. But wouldn't she have resented his unwillingness to cooperate?

"Do you know her brother?"

"I've never seen him."

"Where is he now?"

"Staying with a friend, who's getting married in a couple of weeks and can't keep him any longer."

"Is he young?"

"Younger than his sister—that's all I know. She always refers to him as her little brother."

"What does he do?"

"You'd never guess. He draws cartoons for the papers. That's another lucky thing, because he can work at home."

That had been in the spring, in March or April. Bernard had a memory for weather, though not for time as it went by. Years after an event he could say whether the day had been rainy or sunny, hot or cold, still or blustery. He could see in memory the dead leaves on the trees, or the green buds, whereas he was always in a muddle about dates.

March or April—in this case it didn't matter which. After all, Pierre Mazeron was there now, three floors below the Foys—below their kitchen, to be exact.

At last another bus pulled up, and Nelly leaped out of it, looked up, and waved her right hand; in the other she was carrying a small white package. He waved back, happy of course, relieved that she was home, but disappointed and resentful at the sight of the package.

Usually, Nelly brought nothing back from town, except linen or clothes, and only when they had discussed it beforehand and he had not wanted to shop with her. The food he did not buy, she bought locally, and he would see her going into one shop or another, knowing what she was buying in each and guessing the remarks she was exchanging with the shopkeepers.

Mazeron didn't need his sister to look after him, let alone Nelly. The concierge did his housework, and every day a

31

nurse from the polio after-care center visited him for an hour or two and attended to all his requirements.

Yet nearly every day Gisèle found it necessary to give Nelly a package or a letter, with lengthy instructions, which were probably quite superfluous.

"Will you give this to my brother as you go past? And do tell him that . . . and that . . . and then that . . ." She would ramble on and on, standing on the sidewalk in Place des Victoires, while Bernard dragged out the time at his window.

"You won't forget? You do understand? Thank you, Nelly; you're a sweetie."

That was her favorite word, the reward she handed out to people who did anything for her. They were all sweeties! The old aunt with the varicose veins, who looked after the three children all day and then went home by Métro, although the Lebesques had a car, was a sweetie, too!

He was growing impatient, striding irritably back and forth, and, as he expected, a kind of vacuum was forming in his head. He had tried in vain to describe this feeling to Aubonne, and then to Pellet. They had both asked him, with persistence bordering on disbelief, whether something wasn't upsetting him.

Well, something was at the moment, true enough. His wife's footsteps had stopped on the second floor. He had opened the door a crack to make certain, then closed it again, and the minutes were going by—three, four, five minutes. Did it really take five minutes to give someone a small package?

This was upsetting, yes. But what good would it do to tell the doctors about it? It wouldn't explain anything.

His first bout of dizziness had come in the street, not at home, and at that time Mazeron had not been even a name to him.

And was it true, yes or no, that the X rays showed signs of an old or recent fracture—however microscopic—of his petrosal bone?

He was patient, had been patient all his life. He knew how to wait. He waited for days on end. Too many minutes were going by now, and once again he was on the verge of panic, as he had been when two buses went past and Nelly was not on either of them.

He wasn't angry with her. He had never been angry with her about anything. On the contrary, he was grateful to her and felt daily more astonished at her willingness to live with a man like him without ever a word of complaint.

Sometimes he went further and told himself, sincerely, that he wouldn't have prevented her . . .

She was coming upstairs at last, quickly, almost running, knowing he was waiting, filled with remorse. He let her in. She was out of breath.

"I'm so sorry, but . . ."

He made an effort and smiled at her quite genuinely, since she was there. She kissed him hard on both cheeks.

"It was Gisèle."

"I know."

"Her brother needed various things for his work, I don't know what, exactly. Then I had to tell him she'd been to see the secretary of some magazine editor for him, and what the man had said."

He was watching her closely, but saw no sign of the slightest agitation.

"Have you had a good day?" she asked.

"Not bad."

She didn't ask whether anyone had been to see him, since no one ever came except delivery boys and the men who read the meters.

"Aubonne stopped by."

"Already?"

She seemed truly surprised. "It's only the beginning of the month."

"He's going to Portugal with his wife, partly for a congress and partly on vacation."

She did not say, as he might have feared, "Lucky people!" Much less, of course, "Lucky woman!"

She was thinking only of him. "Did you talk to him about your dizziness?"

"Yes. Or, rather, he talked to me about it."

"What did he say? Wasn't he surprised that it's still happening in spite of the medicine you're taking?"

"I don't think he feels it's very important. No more do I, for that matter."

She was going back and forth between the kitchen and the living room; she put the soup tureen on the table and sat down opposite him. He was still watching her surreptitiously, off and on, because he felt that she was looking at him, too, a little anxiously.

"Did you have any dizzy spells today?"

"Not really. No bad ones."

"You've not been out?"

"No."

She wore her hair neatly nowadays. Her pretty summer dress showed off her more rounded figure. Her face, also rounded, bore no trace of fatigue after the hot day.

"So here you are!" He sighed.

"Did you find the time dragging, too?"

"Luckily, I have something to do."

"How many did you get done?"

"Six. I was working slowly."

"You weren't too hot? The office was stifling, in spite

34

of the fans. And worse for Gisèle, because where she sits there's a glass roof with the sun on it all day long."

He knew Delangle & Abouet from a single visit; everybody had stared at him because of his hooks. They must have felt sorry for Nelly. Maybe that was why he didn't like being seen with her. People were sorry either for him or for her, and, whichever way, he found it unpleasant.

There was no reason to feel sorry for him, at any rate.

"What's he doing?" he asked abruptly.

"Who?"

He couldn't tell whether she really didn't know whom he meant.

"Mazeron."

"Now? I don't know. I suppose he'll soon be having his dinner."

"What was he doing when you went in?"

She hadn't stood at the open door; she'd gone in. He knew the sound of every door in the building. Pellet was grossly mistaken in supposing that he was getting deaf.

"He was reading the evening paper."

"In his wheelchair?"

"Yes. Why?"

"No reason."

He added, with embarrassment: "I know pretty well what everybody in the house is doing. For instance, the Rougins, next door, are having fish for dinner—I saw Madame Rougin buying it at Nau's. She hesitated between mackerel and skate; both were on the slab, and she finally took skate. I concluded that skate was cheaper today, or else the twins don't like mackerel."

She was not deceived by his playful tone, and he felt she was trying to understand the reason for his behavior.

"The little brunette across the street is going to wash her hair; she's put the shampoo out already. As for Mademoiselle Strieb, she gave only two lessons this afternoon, and she has a new pupil who's never touched a piano before."

She laughed.

"You don't get bored, Bernard?"

"Never when you're with me."

"And when I'm not?"

"I wait for you to come back. And since up to now you always have come back . . ."

"Up to now?"

Her brow had puckered.

"Sorry. I was just teasing."

"You're sure?"

"I'm sure. I apologize. Maybe Aubonne's visit annoyed me."

"Why? You like him, and usually you're delighted to see him. What did he say?"

"Nothing in particular. He just looked at me glumly, as though he suspected I was hiding something from him."

"And you aren't?"

"No."

"Nor from me either?"

"Nor from you. Why? What could I be hiding from you?"

"I wonder."

She fetched the salad and the slices of cold meat he had arranged on a dish. He was tempted to seize her hand and say abruptly: "Listen, Nelly . . ."

Then what? What would happen? Nothing! There she was now, sitting opposite him. They were together, in their own home, with the cooler evening air brushing lightly past them from one window to the other. The street noises were becoming less blurred, were beginning to sort themselves out.

"I wonder," said Nelly softly, after hesitating for a long time, "whether we shouldn't go away for a vacation."

"You think so, too?"

"Did Aubonne mention it?"

"He thinks I need a change, that I'm moping, that there's something or other on my mind. I told him it wasn't true, that I'm not happy anywhere except here."

Why did he suddenly feel like weeping? It must be the dusk, after the long day of waiting, and then that little white package that had spoiled everything at the last moment. He was thinking too much. He had too much time to think. In fact, that was probably what the doctor had meant. He was trying to send him somewhere else, no matter where, to give him something new to think about and get him out of his rut.

"What's upsetting you, Bernard?"

She got up and took him by the shoulders while he was screwing his fork into his hook.

"You're unhappy. . . ."

"No, honestly . . ."

"Have I hurt your feelings without knowing it?"

She knew! She knew! It wasn't possible that she didn't realize. But he mustn't tell her, or blame her for it.

"No, honestly . . ." he said again.

Twenty years! He'd had time enough to anticipate everything that might happen, to anticipate the worst, to get used to it. And now . . .

He didn't know, any longer!

"Let's eat," he said, freeing himself.

She sat down again opposite him, and they continued

37

their meal in silence. Nelly kept her eyes on her plate as though afraid to look at him.

After a long pause he muttered, with his mouth half full, "I'm sorry."

She looked up at him with eyes that held a gleam of hope.

Chapter Three

THERE WAS NOTHING very remarkable about that
evening, yet it was one to be filed away in the memory—set apart as though with an intuition that it would
be needed later on.

It was made up of trifles, everyday gestures and words
of no importance, which on that particular evening, heaven
knows why, seemed warmer, more intimate.

The two of them sat at the window on the right, the one
they had adopted when they first moved into the apartment, long before they had any armchairs. The view was
no better than that from the other two windows, but it
had become their special place, and though they could not
hold hands as they used to do in the movie house in Epinal,
they nearly always sat with their knees touching.

They had cleared away and washed the dishes. They had
nothing else to do, and neither of them wanted to read the
paper or listen to the radio.

In the daytime, rue de Turenne was noisy with traffic,

especially buses and many trucks, but now, in the dusk, several minutes would pass between one car and the next, and the few strolling couples could be heard a long way off—their voices rising and falling, with snatches of conversation and now and then a laugh.

Bernard had been right: the brunette across the street had washed her hair, and now she was sitting at the window with an electric drier and reading a magazine that lay in her lap. She was wearing a pink robe. The lamp behind her had a pink shade, too, so the light was pink.

Her neighbor, the man with heart trouble, had dark-green walls in his apartment. He was sitting in a high-backed chair, reading a book; his wife, who had her hair twisted into a tight bun at the back of her head and wore metal-rimmed spectacles, was darning socks.

Three houses farther down, an invisible young man was blowing three hoarse notes every now and then on a muted trumpet—always the same notes, at long intervals, as though he had to pause for breath, or someone was explaining the thing to him. All along the street, people were finishing dinner, children were being put to bed—the twins must be sitting at their homework, one on either side of the table—and the cool of evening was stealing inside after a day that had looked as if it might end in a violent thunderstorm.

It was soothing. Bernard and Nelly sat so still they might have been listening to each other's thoughts. A long time went by before she sighed and said softly, almost timidly, "You wouldn't like a little walk?"

She was probably afraid he would think she was trying to get him out of his rut, like Dr. Aubonne; but that didn't even occur to him. This evening, his suspicions were at rest. He smiled in the darkness and finally stood up, stretching.

"Let's go out."

She helped him on with his jacket. He didn't take his hat and neither did she; she just put a scarf around her shoulders. It was she who locked the door behind them, after making sure the gas was turned off properly.

Unless they were going to the movies, it never occurred to them to turn to the right on leaving the house and go toward Boulevard du Temple and Place de la République— toward town, as they called it, as though their own district did not belong to the city.

They would automatically turn left, and then left again a hundred yards farther on. This brought them under the arcade surrounding Place des Vosges, where footsteps sounded different. The lights looked different too, and here and there shopkeepers were sitting in their doorways.

In the old days, Bernard's father had sat like that, on a straw-bottomed chair, always the same one, to the right of the archway leading into their building. He was a tall, bony man who had come straight here from his village— Drevant, three miles from Saint-Amand-Mont-Rond.

Bernard's mother had been a Mademoiselle Faucher, also from Drevant; his parents had gone to school together before their paths divided, then came together by chance in Paris some years later.

His mother had been general help to a young dentist— in the same district even then, on Boulevard Beaumarchais. His father had driven a heavy wagon, pulled by two horses, for a firm on rue du Caire, and sometimes had deliveries to make around Place de la Bastille.

Bernard remembered him wearing a leather apron and a queer-shaped cap. He had a big, drooping mustache that smelled of red wine. He had been killed in an accident on Boulevard Saint-Michel, crushed between his own wagon and a streetcar.

41

The building where Bernard had been born was on the far side of the central garden around which they were now walking, outside the railings, listening to the sound of the four fountains that had greeted Bernard when he woke in the morning, right through his childhood.

His mother slept in the concierge's lodge, on a folding bed hidden behind a screen; he and his sister slept above, suspended, as it were, between the ground floor and the second floor. The lodge had been divided halfway up, and the upper part was lighted at floor level by the top of the downstairs window.

What did they say to each other on their walk that evening? Almost nothing, nothing important. They paused for a moment outside an antique shop, where the window was still lighted, to look at a big copper basin.

"It's too big for our sideboard," Nelly remarked.

Then they went past Bernard's old school, which at certain hours still released a yelling mob of children into the black-railed central garden.

To his mother, and a great many other people in the district, the rest of Paris had been a foreign city—as it was now to him. He remembered his mother's reply to a stranger who, in search of information, came into the lodge, where he was sitting on the floor:

"It's on the other side of the square, in the Third Arrondissement."

She said it as though referring to a frontier.

He was almost an emigrant, for he had been born in the Fourth, on the Faubourg Saint-Antoine side, and had lived since his marriage in the Third.

It was thoughts such as these that drifted through his mind as he walked at his wife's side.

When they turned into rue de Birague, she asked: "Shall we do the grand tour?"

"You're not tired?"

"No. Are you?"

"Not a bit."

"I don't think there'll be a thunderstorm. . . ."

Clouds were gliding across the moon, which was full and very bright; but they were still reassuringly white, and a few stars could be seen in the distant sky. Every now and then a cool breeze stirred the leaves, like a faint shudder running from one end of the square to the other.

Having decided to do the grand tour, as they called it, they went on along rue de Birague, where in Bernard's childhood two women in full war paint used to take up their station at nightfall outside a hotel with a lighted globe above the entrance. They were always the same two. One was named Irma; she wore a white feather boa around her neck.

Early one morning, when he was about nine years old, the police had surrounded the hotel and organized a real siege, watched from a distance by a few curious spectators, his mother among them.

There had been the sound of shots and of breaking windows. Uniformed police had closed both ends of the street, and two hours went by before a Black Maria drove off with five men and one woman, members of the Polish gang, which was notorious in those days.

Bernard had seen the woman from a distance. Her dress was torn down the front, and she was jeering at the policemen who were pushing her into the van. He had thought her very beautiful. He had also caught a glimpse of a dead man, his head lolling over the side of a stretcher.

They crossed rue Saint-Antoine not far from the lights of the Cinéma Saint-Paul, where he had seen his first film, with no inkling that his fate was to be decided in the darkness of another movie house.

43

"Do you remember Monsieur Félix?" he asked Nelly.

Showing no surprise at the question, she answered: "He still frightens me when I happen to dream about him."

"You dream about him?"

"Sometimes. I'm in Epinal, and I don't know you yet, though I know you exist and that you're supposed to be coming. There's a whole series of obstacles in our way, and my greatest fear is that Monsieur Félix might refuse to let you into his movie house."

"You know what I think about him?"

"No. In those days you used to think he was jealous."

"Because it seemed to me that every man in the place must be in love with you. I still think so at times. The other day he happened to come into my mind. . . ."

"Happened to?"

"Well, I was remembering our first meetings."

"Do you often think about them?"

"If you interrupt all the time, I won't be able to get through what I want to tell you. About Monsieur Félix, I've come to the conclusion that the reason the poor man so often came quietly up behind us, was simply that he was a Peeping Tom.

"You remember?" he added knowingly.

"I wonder how we dared, with so many people around. . . ."

They were going along rue du Petit-Musc, where there was one lighted shop window among the dark buildings; it was the kind of shop found chiefly in the country and in outlying suburbs, with glass jars of candy, piles of dusty-looking cans, and a strange assortment of wares hanging from the ceiling.

Immediately after that they came to the Seine—at Pont de Sully, where they never failed to pause for a moment or two to look at the water flowing by—and finally to the Ile Saint-Louis, around which they slowly strolled.

They had seen the island change, little by little. The house fronts had been cleaned, the entry archways and staircases repainted. A new population had moved in, and for the last few years nearly every time their walk took them there a big party was going on in one house or another, with cars edging onto the sidewalks and uniformed chauffeurs chatting together outside the brilliantly lighted windows.

Sometimes they'd had glimpses of dancing couples, women in low-cut dresses and men in evening clothes. There was music, laughter, the babble of conversation.

No big reception was being held this evening, but in a library, whose walls were lined from floor to ceiling with leatherbound books, a white-haired man in a black velvet jacket sat reading, with a borzoi lying at his feet—just like a picture. There were pictures there, too, old, dark ones, above the door moldings, and a crystal chandelier from which the light fell, bringing out the red of the leather armchair where the reader sat as motionless as though posing for posterity.

"Did you see him?"

"Yes."

No need to say more. They had both registered the picture, which would no doubt remain in their minds as the hallmark, the point of reference, of that particular day.

They stopped again at the prow of the island, opposite the crouching mass of Notre-Dame. Then they started back, across Pont Marie, below which there were barges moored two by two, as though in couples, the yellow light of a lantern gleaming from each deck.

Nelly didn't ask whether he felt dizzy. She wasn't watching him out of the corner of her eye, as she sometimes did in crowds. He was at ease, released, he felt, from the evil thoughts that always made him feel ashamed.

It was when his wife was not with him that those thoughts assailed him. At such times, her behavior, past and present, took on a different meaning.

The most distressing thing about it was that the meaning was always plausible; it tallied with what most people would have thought about her, with what some people undoubtedly did think.

For instance, he saw in his mind's eye the hut where the Rabaud family lived, near the firing range. The father came home drunk every night, and at the slightest whim would beat any of them he could lay his hands on. Bernard had several times noticed bruises on Nelly's body, and she had said to him, with resignation born of habit, "It's nothing. It was my father."

The children slept on straw pallets, with the youngest in a soap box. Fellow-soldiers had assured him that Madame Rabaud had tried to lure them behind a nearby grassy bank. One of them had even bargained with her—just to see, he declared—and told Bernard, laughing, what a ridiculously small sum she had finally agreed to.

"Did you go?"

"I'm not such a fool! They say that last year one of the fellows got something funny to remember her by!"

With Nelly he hadn't been the first. Hadn't she perhaps leaped at the chance to escape from such a degrading life? What did she have to look forward to? Without him, wouldn't she most likely have ended up as a waitress in one of those cafés on the outskirts of town where the girls had to go upstairs with the customers?

Two weeks before he was to be discharged, he had told her: "I must talk to your parents."

46

"Why?"

Didn't she really know? Was she pretending to be innocent?

"To ask their permission to marry you. You're under age. I don't want to go back to Paris alone and come back to get you later on."

Perhaps he'd been afraid that in the meantime someone else might have replaced him.

"But why can't we just go?" she objected.

"Without saying anything?"

"I'll tell them I'm leaving. That's all. Or maybe, so Father won't beat me, I'll leave them a letter. I was eighteen last month; you can't get into any trouble over me."

He could have sworn she'd been making inquiries. When he insisted, she had tried again to make him give up the idea.

"You'll see, they'll ask for money."

"Why?"

"Because I bring in more than I cost them."

She'd had only two dresses in those days, the black one she wore at work and a cotton one she'd bought at the local Monoprix.

Still, he'd gone, one Sunday morning when Rabaud was sleeping off his wine and La Rabaude was bathing the youngest children in a washtub.

"It's him, Mama."

"Oh, so you're the fellow who wants to take my daughter away from me! She swears you mean to make an honest woman of her. Is that true? Can't you be satisfied with a tumble, like the others?"

"It's true, madame."

"And I suppose we're expected to pay for the wedding?"

"We'll be married in Paris, where my mother lives."

"And have you got a job? Soldiers are all the same. They

47

promise, they promise—and afterward it turns out to be just hot air."

However, she had not demanded money. She had merely declared she would not contribute a sou. When Bernard started to go speak to Rabaud, she had dissuaded him.

"You'd better not wait till he wakes up. Sunday mornings, there's no going near him. He'll wake in a bad temper and kick you out."

Did Nelly ever wonder what would have become of her if she hadn't met him? Even in those days, she had been dreaming of tidiness, cleanliness, a little home with well-polished furniture, and an orderly life. Would she have found anyone else to give her all that?

"I'd like to sleep on a barge, at least for one night. To hear the water lapping against the side and feel the boat rise and fall."

They looked down, leaning on the parapet elbow to elbow. Then they walked off along rue Saint-Paul, where two lovers were standing pressed together in a corner.

"Do you remember?" she asked.

They began walking faster. As soon as they were back in the apartment, Nelly drew the curtains, helped her husband undress, and after he had brushed his teeth, took off his prosthesis.

For several years, at the beginning, he had been ashamed of his stumps, especially because the skin had been red, often itchy, and covered with eczema. And he had been ashamed that he couldn't take his wife in his arms, like any other man. He had only half-arms, and without his hooks he couldn't grasp anything.

He lay in his pajamas watching her undress, knowing that sooner or later she would whisper: "Do you want to?"

That was the natural, almost inevitable sequel to the

"grand tour." Nelly's breasts were as firm as a young girl's, and she enjoyed walking around completely naked.

"Do you want to?"

She said it as she turned down the sheet. And he always, as he entered her, felt the same wonderstruck appeasement. At such moments they were really a pair, and he liked to lie still for a long time, crushed tight against her breast, the taste of her saliva in his mouth.

They had no children, though both of them wanted to have some. After two years, Nelly had remarked one day, looking contrite: "It must be me. . . ."

Why her, and not him? He had read in some paper that the cause of a barren marriage rests as often with the husband as with the wife, or even more often. Might not something in his physical makeup have been altered by the shock he had received, or by the treatment he had been given afterward over such a long period?

After all, it had just been discovered, almost accidentally, that a bone in his head, the petrosal bone, had been damaged by that wartime explosion. He had had no trouble from it until twenty years later. Might not some other organ . . .

This was not the moment to bother about such things. They were a pair, one in the other, feeling the same shudders, swept up finally on the crest of the same wave. Before they fell asleep, Nelly lay for some time in the darkness with her head on his chest, as she did every night.

At last she drew away gently and murmured in his ear: "Good night, Bernard."

She was always the first to get up, winter or summer at six o'clock; after twenty years she no longer needed the alarm clock. She would slip noiselessly out of bed and leave the room, carrying her slippers and closing the door carefully behind her. Often he didn't hear her. At other times he was vaguely aware, but his sleep was not really broken.

It was difficult to say which of their habits had originated with her and which with him. Some of them went back to the very beginning; others had gradually been added, forming a tradition they never thought of changing.

Getting up at six o'clock had been insisted upon by Nelly, even before she went to Delangle & Abouet. It started during the war, when she was working at Florence Nussbaum's, making artificial flowers.

The workshop had been in an old building on rue Coquillière, with dark, rambling passageways, off which were many artisans' shops. She had to be at work by eight-thirty every morning.

Bernard was still having pain and found it hard to get used to the different devices the doctors and orthopedists were trying out on him, one after another.

It had been a difficult time—a dark period, in the sense in which the Middle Ages in his history book had been dark. He had found it hard to believe that the period of nobles' castles could have been more sinister than in those illustrations; he had been particularly impressed by the ones that showed instruments of torture, or four horses quartering a man.

He had been glad to be alive, to have found Nelly, when so many people were scattered far and wide; glad, too, that she had not looked at him with fear or horror—or with pity, which would have hurt him even more.

As long as he was in the hospital or at the rehabilitation center, he had not thought about what life would be like when he went home. They said to him: "The latest prostheses are so efficient that with a little patience and determination you'll be able to do as much with them as you used to with your hands."

This was partly true, partly false. For one thing, his temporary hooks gave him almost unbearable pain, and Aubonne used to come every other day to cheer him up and try to find out what was wrong.

The big-headed doctor had been his first piece of good luck; he owed his life to him. His second stroke of luck had come when, quite by accident, he had gone to see the bearded old orthopedist on rue du Chemin-Vert, although the people at the rehabilitation center spoke of him slightingly.

The occupation was dragging on. The most up-to-date prostheses were American, German, or Swiss, and thus unobtainable.

"Later on we'll fit you with the new active grip, or even a hand with an automatic thumb."

He could remember the brochures showing plastic hands that from a distance might have been taken for real ones. He had refused them.

Years later they had shown him jointed hands with electro-pneumatic controls that made it possible to move certain fingers at will.

But old Hélias had fitted him with the plain metal hooks available then, to which he made cautious improvements, week by week.

"Let them talk, my boy, and don't you believe a word they say. It'll take two years to find out what kind suits you best."

He used to wake up with a start in the night, feeling pain in his missing fingers, and while Nelly got him a tranquilizer he would lie moaning, bathed in sweat.

"This is no life for you," he would say, pitying her. "I'm a dead weight. It would have been better . . ."

"Stop it, you idiot!"

For weeks he had refused to make love to her, convinced she must find him repulsive. He could clearly remember the evening when, laughing defiantly, she had literally raped him.

"There! Now do you understand?"

One morning Nelly had arrived at the workshop on rue Coquillière to find the door locked. The concierge told her the Germans had just taken Florence Nussbaum away.

The Foys had no money, and everything was expensive. For several weeks Nelly worked as a waitress in a small restaurant; then she had found a job as clerk with Delangle & Abouet.

"At least let me do the housework," he had begged her.

She was thin; her eyes were dark-ringed. She was working too hard and not getting enough to eat.

"Anything else you like—the cooking, if you insist—but never the housework."

He was beginning to use his pincers at that time, and could change his knife for a spoon, fork, or another of the ingenious gadgets old Hélias was making for him.

Hélias wore the yellow star, as Florence Nussbaum had, and Bernard was afraid the old man would be deported, just as she was. Luckily, the shop was so dark and uninviting, and the old man so seldom emerged from it, that he was overlooked.

For the Liberation celebration, they wanted Bernard to parade with a couple of hundred other men who had lost limbs; but he refused to display his stumps on the Champs-Elysées, and he never joined any of the associations that were formed afterward.

Thanks to them, however, he got a pension, which steadily increased, until it was finally equal to ordinary wages. Nelly went on working, and he set to work himself, to fill up the day. Aubonne had advised him to do so.

The reason he had elected to paint flowers on metal-and-parchment lampshades was that an old spinster who once lived in his mother's house had earned her living that way. Hélias made him some special pincers, wonderfully adaptable, to hold his brushes.

Thus they had gradually got organized, and the apartment acquired more furniture and began to take on an air of prosperity.

More often than not, he was awakened in the morning by the smell of coffee as the door opened and Nelly called out cheerfully: "Time to get up!"

She kissed him. The whole apartment was already spick and span. After his bath, which she helped him to take, she put on his prosthesis, a complicated system of straps around his neck and shoulders, by means of which he could adjust the movable parts of the hooks.

"Breakfast's ready!"

In their life as a married couple there had never been a day when they had actually chosen their respective places at the table, but for the last twenty years neither would have dreamed of changing. The croissants were hot, and the newspaper lay on the arm of his chair near the window.

"Did you sleep well?" she would ask.

"I went off almost immediately, and only woke once."

"Did you get up?"

"Yes."

"I never heard you."

At that hour of the day only a thin ray of sunshine came in through the window overlooking rue des Minimes. The news was coming softly over the radio. The old couple opposite were at breakfast, too, and the twins banged the door of the next apartment and rushed downstairs. Out in the street they set off at a run, still shouting.

Bernard would have liked to make this part of the day last longer, but Nelly glanced at the clock every now and then. He wound that clock himself; she never touched it. Ever since his childhood he had longed for a clock with a brass pendulum, and the day he had been able to afford one was a red-letter day in his life.

Every morning when the eight o'clock time signal came over the radio, he would automatically get up to push the hands back or forward, even if only by a millimeter.

"What would you like for lunch?"

"I'll do the shopping today," he replied.

"Why?"

"I don't know. Maybe because Dr. Aubonne advised me to get around more."

This was not true, and his wife must suspect as much. He had not done the shopping for the last two weeks, and he had evaded every pretext for getting him out of doors. Today he had decided not to spend the whole time cooped up. Or, rather, the previous evening he had resolved to shake off his evil thoughts, once and for all.

"So it's my turn to ask you what you'd like for lunch."

"What day is it?"

"Tuesday."

"That's the day the butcher has liver. Would it be too much trouble to cook some?"

"I'll even do some extra, so we can have it cold another time."

He was happy, playful. This was the beginning of a lovely day, without a cloud in the sky, and the sparrows were chirping merrily, coming right to the window to beg for crumbs. Nelly looked cool and pretty in a close-fitting dress with blue spots; it set off the neat curves of her waist and behind.

He had kept a kind of aftertaste of last night's love-making, and watched her with quiet gratitude as he sipped his coffee.

In theory, coffee was taboo for him, like wine and alcohol, but Aubonne allowed him one cup in the morning. Sometimes—today, for instance—he broke the rule and poured himself a second cup, to show that he was happy, to make an even more perfect beginning for the day.

"I love you, madame," he said suddenly, smiling at his wife.

"And I love you, monsieur. Isn't that a lucky coincidence?"

This was a game they played from time to time.

"I have a good mind," he went on, "to go downstairs with you, like a real gentleman, and see you off on the bus."

His eyes were still laughing. Nelly's, too, had been sparkling, up to that moment; now a look of hesitation came into them, and that was enough to worry him. Still, he tried to keep up the joke.

"Would my company be displeasing to you, madame?"

"On the contrary, monsieur . . ."

The tone was no longer the same, in spite of their efforts. It had lost its lightness.

"Only, I have to stop on the way. . . ."

Seeing her husband's gloomy face, she dropped the game and went on in a different tone, laying her hand on his shoulder: "I was going to tell you as I left. Gisèle's brother . . ."

He noticed she did not call him Mazeron, or Pierre—as though she was avoiding any suspicion of intimacy.

"Gisèle's brother had some urgent drawings to finish last night. She is to take them to the paper at lunchtime. . . ."

"And you're to stop and pick them up?"

"What could I do? You know what she's like. With her, everything's always desperately important. I hadn't thought that just this morning . . ."

He gulped down the coffee he had been meaning to enjoy slowly, stood up, and went over to his armchair, where he unfolded the newspaper on his knees.

"You're cross?"

"No."

"Unhappy?"

"No. I don't know. I'm sorry. . . ."

He added, after glancing at the clock: "Time you started, if you have to stop on the way . . ."

"It won't take a second. Just a roll of drawings to pick up. I needn't even go in. . . ."

"Run along."

"Listen, Bernard . . ."

"Run along, dear. Don't make yourself late."

He was on the point of adding bitterly: "Don't worry, I won't forget the liver!"

But he choked back the words and pretended to begin reading. She bent down and gave him a lingering embrace. There was a sad, pleading look in her eyes.

"Try to be happy, Bernard. Never mind about Gisèle—I won't go!"

"I want you to go."

"You insist?"

"Yes."

"Look at me."

He did so, struggling to hide the nightmare that was assailing him again.

She had to go now. People who work seldom have time to talk things out thoroughly.

"Run along . . . I promise I'll . . ."

He got up a little later to watch her standing on the opposite sidewalk, under the green sign that marked the bus stop. She returned his gaze with equal intensity; before getting in the bus she waved, and he waved back.

Then he was alone with his thoughts again, and already feeling the discomfort that preceded his attacks of dizziness. . . .

Chapter Four

HE WENT DOWNSTAIRS slowly, touching the railing now and then to reassure himself, almost like the man opposite, with the bad heart, who always seemed about to cling to the buildings he passed. Upstairs, he had determined not to pause on the second floor; but he couldn't resist doing so, telling himself that it was in order to recover his balance.

The door on one side of the landing was newly varnished; it had a thick, red-edged mat, and an enamel plate with the name F. Jussieu—Fernand or François or Ferdinand or Frédéric; he didn't know which. The opposite door was shabby and had no mat and no plate, not even a card stuck up with a tack.

What fascinated Bernard was the white china doorknob, which he had never touched, but which Nelly had often turned, including that very morning.

He didn't remember ever seeing that door open when old Monsieur François lived in the apartment, and he had only a vague idea what lay behind it. All he knew was that there were two rooms, one quite tiny and the other fairly large, looking over the courtyard, so it got no sun.

The new tenant never opened the door himself. When anyone knocked he called "Come in!" in a voice that sounded far off.

Nelly had been in, not only this morning, but also yesterday evening and on many other occasions. That made one more place and one more face that she knew well and that Bernard didn't know at all.

Nor did he know everyone at Place des Victoires, where he had gone only for that one brief visit several years ago. Almost every day she mentioned the names of men and women whose doings became quite familiar to him although he wouldn't have recognized them in the street.

He had never been jealous of those people; yet now he was hypnotized by a door, by an ivory-white china knob, to such an extent that he was tempted to feel it with the tip of his hook.

It was as though he was hurt by Nelly's knowing what he did not. He went on downstairs. He had paused for only a few seconds, but he felt guilty when the concierge opened her glass door as he went by.

"A letter for you, Monsieur Bernard."

She was the same concierge who had been there when he moved in, and she always asked for news of his mother, whom she used to know well. She had known his father, too.

"Such a fine man! Looked as if he'd live to be a hundred!"

From a distance he recognized the yellow envelope and the type; it came from an association for the war-disabled. They kept inviting him to meetings, though he'd never set

60

foot in the place. He had had no great difficulty in accepting the fact that he would be disabled for the rest of his life, a life that would have to be different from other people's; but he refused to settle down into a separate world, meeting other men as diminished as he was, who would talk about their difficulties, their medals, their pensions, and their rights.

"And how have you been, Monsieur Bernard?"

"Very well, thank you."

She glanced at him once too often and too hard, it seemed to him, and then felt impelled to ask again, "Are you really all right?"

Did that mean he looked ill, or depressed? He wasn't in the throes of an attack—not yet. He felt only a little hazy, from the unsteady sensation he was beginning to know so well.

This was what Pellet called his vertiginous condition, to distinguish it from the actual dizzy spells. According to the doctor, Bernard did not suffer from real vertigo, and it was true that he never fell down in the street or was unable to go a step farther. And—again according to Pellet—although he sometimes leaned against a wall, he did so not because of any physical necessity, only because of an unfounded fear.

"Off to do the shopping?"

Until a few months, or even a few weeks ago, a round of the local shops was one of the things he enjoyed most, and he was not in the least embarrassed to set out with a basket or a net bag, like a housewife. In the shops, where he often had to wait his turn, he met few men, and those few were nearly all old—pensioners, widowers, unsociable diehards, or husbands with bedridden wives.

He began with the butcher, since later in the morning

the liver might be sold out. The sun was glaring down on the sidewalk, the red ironwork, and the red-and-yellow-striped canvas stretched out across the marble window slab in summer, making it difficult for the customers to squeeze through.

Inside, it was pleasantly cool, and women's faces, expressionless in the semidarkness, turned silently toward him as one. That happened whenever anybody came in. He knew all the women by sight, and knew where most of them lived.

On the sawdust-covered floor thick patches of blood were coagulating below the sides of beef that hung from hooks. Even the rather sickly smell of meat was not disagreeable, he found.

"And for you, Madame Blanc?"

In a whisper, as though ashamed to admit that she was poor and all alone, she answered: "A small steak, please. Not more than a quarter of a pound."

The butcher's name was Désiré Lenfant. He had huge hairy forearms, and his wife, at the cash register, had a round, pink countrywoman's face and a vast bosom, pushed up toward her chin by her bra.

Lenfant turned to her and called out a price; then, to the customers: "Next, please."

There were those who, like Madame Blanc, asked timidly for a small piece and those who were buying for two; there were also young mothers, often carrying a baby, sometimes with a little girl or boy clinging to their skirt, and they might need six, seven, or eight portions. Nearly all of them had drawn features and bowed shoulders, and they were likely to choose stew meat.

Those who left were replaced by new arrivals, and everybody moved on one place each time. In spite of the striped canvas that shut out the sun, flies were buzzing. But a breath of cooler air wafted from the refrigerator whenever the assistant went there to get a larger piece of meat.

"For you, Monsieur Foy?"

"A pound and a half of liver."

"Is there any liver left, Hubert?"

"Yes, sir."

"Shall I cut it up for you?"

"No. I'll take it in one piece, but I'd like you to lard it."

Lenfant gave him a knowing glance.

"And how are you these days?"

"Very well, thank you."

Why did people seem not to believe him? The butcher was looking at him doubtfully. Whenever a dizzy spell came on, Bernard felt as though he turned pale, and had staring eyes and tight-pressed lips; but Nelly, who had several times seen him going through one, declared it wasn't so.

"I assure you, you look very well."

Once or twice he had looked at himself in a shop window, but it was hard to judge.

There had been four people waiting when he came in, and now there were four behind him, all staring at him, perhaps automatically. Everybody, especially the children, watched in fascination as he took the bills and coins out of his purse, using his pincers with the adroitness of a juggler.

What did they say when he'd gone? Probably Lenfant would grunt: "He's been in a bad way lately."

And someone would be sure to remark: "In his condition he's lucky to have such a pretty young wife!"

"Is it true he does all the housework?"

"Not at all! From my window I can see his wife cleaning every morning at six o'clock."

"Was he like that when she married him?"

"I couldn't say. They came to live here before we did."

"I know. They'd just got married when the war began. His mother was a concierge on Place des Vosges."

"He must get a big pension."

He was making up a conversation he was sure could not be far from the truth as he went to the dairy. It had white marble shelves and counter, and a pair of beautiful copper scales.

"And for you, Monsieur Foy? What do you fancy today? I've got some Brie just the way your little lady likes it."

Although the proprietress did not ask after his health, she threw him a curious glance. Was he imagining things this morning? People seemed to think he looked poorly, or to be feeling sorrier than usual for him and making a special effort to be nice.

"You don't feel the heat too much up there, with the sun on your windows nearly all day? Of course you're at the corner, so you can always get a draft. . . ."

Finally he went to Bourre's, the grocery. He didn't need a list; he remembered everything they'd run out of or would soon be needing—peppercorns, mustard, sugar, metal polish. The coffee would last another two or three days. He preferred to buy small quantities, so that it was always freshly roasted.

On his way upstairs he nearly had an opportunity to look through that door. The white-uniformed nurse had gone into the building just ahead of him. He followed her upstairs, seeing her legs to above the knee. Her hips moved nimbly, lightly. She was fresh as a daisy, quick and gay as a kitten.

If he had hurried, he would have reached the landing almost at the same time she did. But after knocking, as a formality, she opened the door without waiting, and he had only time for a glimpse of a yellow wall and a patch of ceiling.

At once he heard them talking cheerfully. When he reached his own apartment and put down his basket in the kitchen, he was bathed in sweat.

He peeled onions, made a bouquet garni, and buttered the bottom of the stew pan. Once he had finished and put it on the gas, he went back to the living room; he would have nothing more to do in the kitchen for some time. Not having the energy to begin painting lampshades, he released a curtain the breeze had hooked on the window catch, started to switch on the radio, didn't do so, and finally subsided into his armchair.

It was, presumably, from moments like this that Dr. Aubonne had wanted to rescue him by sending him on vacation, no matter where. He was depressed, true enough—he admitted it to himself. But not all the time, not all day. His frame of mind was like his attacks of dizziness: both left him in peace for hours on end. There had been yesterday evening, and today had begun well, too. It should have been a splendid day. If it hadn't been for . . .

He could hardly say what had ruined it for them. An insignificant word, just when his wife and he had been in their most playful mood. It hadn't been Nelly's fault. It was Gisèle, with her passion for making use of people.

It was Gisèle. . . .

But had it really been Gisèle? That was the snag, the thing he couldn't confess to Dr. Aubonne or anyone else. In the first place, did people realize that he wasn't leading a man's life?

In their household, the roles were reversed. It was his wife who went off to work in the morning, came back at lunchtime steeped in the life outside, left again afterward, and didn't get home till evening.

And what about him, meanwhile? He stayed at home like most wives; waited, cooked the stewed liver—he must take care not to let it burn.

He could while away the time by saying to himself, after a glance at the clock, "Nelly's doing this. . . . Nelly's doing that. . . ."

But what did he really know about it? Wives who stayed at home all day must surely sometimes feel the same doubts about their husbands. But they were women, and they were not diminished by the loss of both hands. They could take their men in their arms when they came home, and walk along the street beside them without attracting pitying glances from others.

Just the same, didn't they suffer from the same kind of jealousy that came over him at times? Didn't they sometimes sniff at the homecomer, seeking for an alien smell?

It was nothing new. He had been through these distressful periods earlier, particularly in the first few years, when his stumps were a persistent purplish color and he was convinced he would never learn to use the hooks.

Since he could do nothing without Nelly, he had felt as weak and helpless as a baby in her hands. As for her, she had married a man, and what she needed was a man.

It was a real, almost excruciating need; he knew that. He had discovered it with some surprise, to tell the truth. Sometimes he had been awakened during the night by the bed shaking, and when he switched on the lamp he had found her lying beside him in what seemed a state of terror.

At first he used to ask, "What's the matter?"

"Nothing, Bernard . . . I had a dream. . . ."

Little by little she had confessed that these dreams were

invariably passionate, erotic, and with vivid detail that astounded him. She declared that they were about him, that it was he, certain parts of his body, that came before her in her sleep. Was that true? Was it possible to become so excited about a man who was maimed?

He did not blame her. He had never blamed her for anything and he never would, whatever happened. He couldn't have said when this was exactly, but it was soon after the Liberation. It seemed as though Paris was suddenly coming fully alive again, happiness was being reborn, and youth restored to its rights.

Life was a succession of festivities, dancing, and sunlit processions, and the American soldiers were chasing girls in the streets. There was sex in the very air one breathed, and they had sometimes turned aside to avoid a couple making love against one of the pillars on Place des Vosges.

About then he had felt inclined to say to her: "You know, Nelly, you're free. . . ."

It would have cost him a pang, but he felt that honesty required it of him. He had no right to condemn a young woman, overflowing with life, to his own withdrawn existence.

He would still be her husband, her companion, the man she loved. She would come back to him every time. She would come back every evening. He would ask no questions. She wouldn't tell him anything. They would be happy, trusting, like a real couple, and therefore he would still have his share, in spite of everything.

He would prefer her not to take a lover, just different men, strangers as far as possible, and he would not have let her see he was unhappy about it.

After all, that would be better than being dead, or losing her altogether.

It was he, not she, who'd been called up and who had touched off a mine while playing at Boy Scouts in the snow. It was he who'd been given a medal when he didn't know exactly what had happened. There was no reason she should suffer for it!

In actual fact, he had never said any of this to her. Then, as now, such ideas had come to him on certain days, at certain hours, and he had been quick to dismiss them.

In those days he had sometimes wondered, too, whether she had waited for his permission to go with American soldiers, or with no matter whom.

When he'd been working at the garage in the central markets, she had sometimes taken two or three days off— for instance, that week they'd scraped the walls of the apartment and repapered them. And she'd managed to be free whenever they had something important to do—papers to be signed somewhere for his pension, say—or if they simply felt a need to be together for a time during the day.

She went off to Delangle & Abouet every morning, of course. But what proof had he that at this very moment she was in the office on Place des Victoires?

He felt like taking a sheet of paper, drawing a line down the middle, writing *For* at the head of one column and *Against* at the head of the other, and making out a kind of balance sheet. The first thing he'd write, at the top, yet again, would be that he didn't blame her, that he had no right to. Perhaps he would also put down an idea that occurred to him fairly often, which he'd never allowed anybody to suspect—her least of all, of course. Would a man like Dr. Aubonne, who saw all kinds of people and must hear some strange confessions, be able to understand it?

I wish she were ugly!

If she were ugly, he'd love her just as much, if not more, and other men wouldn't turn to stare at her. He would be the one to be pitied when they walked down the street together.

Ugly or disfigured!

He had also said to himself, long ago: "When she's forty, men won't want her anymore."

She was now thirty-eight and more desirable than ever. Not only to him. He saw it in other men's faces as they went by.

He'd like to begin with the *Against* column, in order to get it over quickly, and because that was the most distressing part—so much so that he usually broke off this train of thought without following it to its conclusion.

Would that column include Nelly's dreams, on the assumption that her excitement did not spring from memories of his own pitiful embraces?

She was meeting men all day long, and at Delangle & Abouet they weren't all old fogeys. He was prepared to ignore the bookkeepers, who were all staid, middle-aged men.

The firm made braid and other trimmings; it was the largest in that trade, not only in Paris but also in France, perhaps in Europe. Orders and buyers arrived there from all over the world.

Monsieur Delangle was seventy-nine. They would soon be celebrating his eightieth birthday; his only daughter lived in Switzerland with her husband and children.

Monsieur Abouet was just over fifty, and his eldest son— Monsieur Jean-Paul, as Nelly called him—had recently joined the firm.

"What sort of man is he?"

"He spent three years in a silk factory in Lyon before

his father made him assistant manager. Now he runs the foreign department, because he speaks several languages. They say he intends to modernize the whole place."

That didn't tell him what the fellow was like.

"Is he married?"

"Yes. I've seen his wife only once. She's tall and fair, rather pretty. They live on Boulevard Suchet and have an expensive sports car."

"Is he fair too?"

"No, darkish . . ."

She seemed to be trying to remember.

"Yes . . . darkish."

"Where's his office?"

"On the second floor, next to Monsieur Delangle's. When Monsieur Delangle retires, he'll take his place. For the time being, he travels a lot."

Wasn't it only natural for her to talk like that about men she worked with, with whom she spent almost more time than with him—much more time if you didn't count the hours of sleep?

She saw no harm in it, no doubt, not realizing that words did not sound the same to a man whose days were spent waiting for her, as to a woman who lived in the center of things.

Perhaps this Jean-Paul had a crooked nose, wore thick glasses, had an ugly twist to his mouth. Perhaps he was a young martinet, or thought it beneath him to notice a member of his staff.

Unlikely. Nelly spoke of him in a rather friendly way. But she did this about everything connected with Place des Victoires.

That saddened him, too. Nelly felt at home in places other than their apartment. She was used to the office, had her own chair there, a hook for her coat, a drawer for her personal belongings. She told the time by another clock, an electric clock he had noticed in passing, and it was as though she lived by a different time from him.

Was it before or after Jean-Paul's arrival that she had been promoted to be head of a department? For several months now she had been a person of importance in the firm. From one day to the next, people had stopped calling her Nelly—except for close friends like Gisèle, she had become Madame Foy.

She now ruled over the big sample room on the second floor, near the managers' offices, a room paneled in light oak, with shelves that held thousands of ticketed samples. She had five women under her, most of them young girls, but one about fifty, though it was true she had joined the firm long after Nelly, who'd been there longer than anyone except the chief bookkeeper and the sample-room supervisor.

Perhaps that might go in the *For* column.

Had she been promoted soon after Jean-Paul came in as assistant manager? He couldn't remember. Besides, she might not necessarily have mentioned young Abouet the very day he arrived in the place. She sometimes said things like: "By the way, last week one of the truck drivers . . ."

Wasn't it about then that she'd ordered three dresses all at once? She no longer bought them ready-made; she had found a dressmaker who worked well for her and wasn't expensive—Madame Levart, on rue de Sévigné, opposite the girls' school.

When she went for a fitting at the end of the day, Bernard would go to the door with her and then stroll up and down, waiting. She wanted him to come upstairs.

"You can tell me what you think. . . ."

He had gone twice, and Madame Levart had insisted on offering him a glass of vermouth, which he had not dared refuse.

It was he who had wanted his wife to think more about her appearance and get some new clothes.

"We go out so seldom, Bernard. . . ."

"It's not because of other people that I want you to be nicely dressed."

On the face of it, it was he who'd made her order the three dresses. But in previous springs he had urged her in the same way, and she had never gone further than buying one or two dresses and altering old ones.

Moreover, this time, and without his having to suggest it, she had bought two handbags, gloves, and shoes to go with one of the dresses, a thing that had never happened before.

She'd even remarked: "I've begun to realize that a woman takes more interest in her appearance as she grows older. That's when she most needs to, of course. Has it occurred to you that in a very few years I'll be an old woman? I so much want you to go on thinking I'm pretty! You know, Bernard, it's for you that . . ."

He had felt like saying sharply: "No. It's for yourself!"

Or for some other man. Or for other men. He didn't know. He was reduced to guessing. Everything seemed possible; everything was likely.

Even the fact that with maturity she was becoming more beautiful, more desirable, made him uneasy. A woman head over heels in love becomes more radiant than ever, they say.

As for *his* love, she had long been accustomed to that. The little usherette in Epinal had not bothered about clothes or her appearance. She'd been in love, and that was all. She thought of Bernard's love for her as something permanent, and used no stratagems to keep it alive.

She had even changed her hairdresser lately! The new one had cut off the two unruly locks Bernard was so fond of, above her ears.

"I was furious!" she'd said. "I'd specially told him not to change anything. It hadn't occurred to me to watch what he was doing. I looked away for a moment at a woman who came in, and that was that."

For or against? More against, wasn't it? Knowing he wanted her to keep those two locks . . . and that he liked her to be as unaffected as possible.

"You see, now I have to deal with the salesmen, and everyone calls me Madame Foy. . . ."

If he hadn't lost his hands, if he'd gone on working at the garage, if he'd become foreman or even assistant manager, wouldn't he have exchanged his coveralls for a well-cut suit and been more careful about shaving?

The most serious problem was Mazeron. When the question came up about asking the concierge to give him Monsieur François's apartment, Bernard had asked: "What's he like, this fellow?"

Always the same question, about every man. Wasn't it natural?

"I've never seen him."

"Doesn't he ever come to Place des Victoires to see his sister?"

He thought she hesitated before answering. And wasn't her reply ambiguous?

"He may have come before he had polio. I don't know. Gisèle and I aren't in the same department."

Yet she knew every detail of the lives of the girls she

worked with, and even of the young women in the front office and the firm's salesmen.

That had been in the spring, in March or April.

Suppose she'd known Pierre Mazeron a long time already? It was by no means impossible. Gisèle had been working at Delangle & Abouet for five or six years. They had become friends at once. She might have introduced her brother to Nelly some evening, as they left the shop. Why shouldn't she have said to him: "You'll see! She's quite pretty, and her figure isn't at all bad. She doesn't have much of a life. She's married to a cripple who never goes out or takes her anywhere."

It was not the first time this idea had come into his mind. Usually he dismissed it. When he'd been working in the garage, one of the apprentices, not knowing he was married, had suggested to him one evening, "You wouldn't care to go out with my young sister, would you?"

No! He drove that thought from his mind. She had no doubt made his acquaintance only after Gisèle had asked her about an apartment. Hadn't she gone to see him then— with Gisèle, perhaps—to give him the good news?

He got up and went to turn the liver; its savory smell was spreading through their rooms. His movements were still calm and deft. Standing at the sink, he began peeling potatoes and slicing carrots into rounds; he would add these half an hour before his wife came home.

"No!" he said under his breath.

Again he dismissed the thought. She had never met Mazeron until he moved in downstairs.

But since then? At least every other day there was a package or a letter to give him from Gisèle. That was perfectly true. Gisèle and her husband had come up to the apartment one Sunday when they'd come to see Mazeron.

Nelly had brought out vin rosé and biscuits, takin
trouble, as though eager to please them. Why?

Gisèle had said to Bernard in the course of the
sation: "I wonder how you managed to find yours
a wife! She's a sweetie!"

She had added, in what seemed quite a natur
"Sometimes I feel ashamed of exploiting her. But
brother is so lonely! If people didn't lend him a
don't know how he would manage. You know
like; you're in somewhat the same position."

It was perhaps those words that had stung hi
with their comparison between him and the you
his wife visited nearly every day.

"He's so grateful to her for taking all that tr
find him a place to live. . . ."

That wasn't true. Nelly had taken no trouble.
simply asked the concierge, perhaps adding a
behalf of Gisèle's brother. Or else she had lied to

What was left of the *Against* column? He did
know; he preferred to stop thinking about it. It wo
be time to set the table, wash the salad greens, a
his usual small chores.

Actually, he could fill one column as logical
other, depending on his mood and how confiden
pened to be feeling. For years he had had no s
about his wife, and his only concern had been to
as happy as he could.

Why, all of a sudden, at the age of forty-two,
often feel he hadn't succeeded?

He turned on the radio without thinking abou
he usually listened to music while working at
shades. He was just putting the slice of Brie on a
he jumped, almost in alarm. He, who heard ev

75

n the building, and the street noises at the same time, had
heard nothing at all; yet Nelly was there, with her arms
around his shoulders.

"What . . ." he began.

Through the open door he could see the clock in the
living room; it said ten minutes to twelve. That wasn't his
wife's usual time, and she was not behaving in the usual
way. She had taken his face between her hands and was
kissing him on the cheeks, the forehead, the mouth, her
eyes full of anxiety.

"What . . ." he said again, baffled.

He hadn't finished driving away his bad thoughts, and
he felt worried by Nelly's excitement and her unexpected
return.

"I couldn't wait till twelve o'clock," she was saying. "If
you knew what a dreadful morning I've had . . ."

"Why?"

"Can't you guess?"

He stubbornly remained on the defensive, as though
sulking.

"It's the first time we ever parted like that. . . ."

"I waved to you from the window," he protested.

"I don't dare tell you all the ideas that went through
my head. . . . We were so happy last evening! I hadn't seen
you so relaxed for weeks. And this morning, too. It reminded me a little of when we first moved in here. And
then it had to . . ."

"Please don't say any more about it."

She looked searchingly at him, her face more serious.

"You've had a bad morning, too, haven't you?"

He merely shrugged his shoulders.

"A dizzy spell?"

He was going back and forth obstinately, finishing set-

76

ting the table, keeping his back to her most of the time.

"Bernard!"

"Yes?"

"Are you really so jealous that it makes you unhappy, ill? Are you imagining I might be interested in some other man?"

"I don't know. Perhaps not."

"Perhaps?"

"Why should I be the only man in the world?"

"And you? Could you . . . ?"

She checked herself at once.

"You're a man. It's not the same thing."

"What did you say to Monsieur Jean-Paul?"

"I told him I'd forgotten I had a dentist's appointment."

She had lied. She could lie.

"I went to speak to Gisèle," she continued. "I asked her not to give me any more messages for her brother. . . ."

"Why did you do that? . . . What excuse did you give her?"

"I didn't mention you. I said the other tenants might begin to talk. . . ."

"What did she say?"

"Nothing. She'll just stop calling me a sweetie!"

He laughed in spite of himself, still holding the salad bowl.

"Do put that down, you idiot," she said abruptly, "so I can get close and hug you. . . ."

They were both crying. It was the first time they had shed tears together.

Chapter Five

IN TWENTY YEARS they had never come so close to each other as on that afternoon—as close, they both felt, as two human beings could ever be.

Yet scarcely had those hours gone—hours without pretense or formality, hours that seemed cut off from the world, hours when everything became different, when their bodies and souls were more sensitive, when they spoke as though in a fever—scarcely had that time gone by when they were toppling over into the past.

What would remain of them next day, and the following days? What would remain of them in a few months or a few years?

Pictures had imprinted themselves, unbidden; tones and glances had been caught by chance, even sounds from outside, which had made a kind of background music to their encounter.

Would they ever forget the half-empty bottle of red wine standing on the table, which looked as though it were cut into two bleeding pieces because a ray of sunshine was sparkling right in the middle of it? And the plates, with a little gravy left on them, scraps of bread lying there, and four untouched apples on a dish?

Bernard had drunk more than his usual half-glass of wine. Two or three glasses, perhaps four; his eyelids were hot, and he could feel them fluttering. Nelly, in an undertone, was telling him about her morning, how she had almost got off the bus right away, at the first stop, and hurried home.

They were still avoiding each other's eyes, from a kind of bashfulness. They did not want the conversation to get too emotional, and anybody watching them—the woman opposite, maybe—might have thought they were chatting about unimportant things.

"All the time I was at work, I never took my eyes off the clock. I was trying to follow you in my mind, telling myself that now you'd be doing the shopping, now you'd be going upstairs again. I wanted to imagine your face, and I couldn't do it. I think that was what upset me most."

Just like him, not only that morning, but on other mornings, other afternoons.

"Finally I couldn't stand it any longer, so I made up the story about the dentist."

"What were you afraid of?"

"That you might be unhappy . . . That you might be moping . . ."

"You were afraid I'd have an attack of dizziness?"

"Aubonne set my mind at rest about that. No—it was the idea that I'd hurt you without meaning to. It was only little by little that I began to understand. You're really jealous, Bernard?"

He nodded, regretfully.

"So you're still in love?"

"I love you."

"After all these years?"

"What about you? Are you getting tired of living with me, after so long?"

"You know I'm not."

"How would I know?"

"Listen! I'll tell you what I'm going to do. I don't feel like going back to work today. I want to stay with you. I'll call and tell them I had a bad time at the dentist's, that he had to give me a painkiller and advised me to go to bed."

They didn't have a telephone. What use would it have been? They had nobody, really, to call and nobody to call them. They might have talked to each other during the hours of separation, of course; but Delangle & Abouet employees were not allowed to make or receive private calls.

She went down right after lunch, and he saw her walk into the Café de Turenne, opposite the pastry shop, where there was a public telephone.

Unlike other days, he did not clear the table; after wandering around as though in search of a corner in which to settle, he went to lie down on the bed.

He would have found it difficult later to describe his state of mind and body. He remembered a word he had read somewhere and had not quite understood at the time. Today he applied it to him: he felt dolorous.

It was not disagreeable. A dull, voluptuous ache was penetrating deeply into his flesh, and he wanted to lance this abscess. He wanted to talk to Nelly, to tell her all the things he'd never told her, to rid himself in one burst of the confused, crawling mass of evil thoughts that had been visiting him more and more often.

He did not know how to do it, whether he could. He

was afraid that in selfishly shaking off a burden that was growing too heavy, he might simply pass it to his wife.

He heard her come upstairs and open the front door. Not seeing him in the living room, she would certainly glance, anxiously, into the kitchen before coming to their bedroom.

It was as though she, too, were living on tiptoe, aware that they were precariously balanced and that the slightest clumsy word or gesture might hurt them badly.

"Shall I close the curtains?"

The bedroom window looked onto rue des Minimes, and a pair of pink panties, a bra, and a slip were hung up to dry on a line stretched across an attic window just opposite.

"Close the curtains, but leave the window open."

He didn't want to be completely cut off from the world; he didn't want them to feel shut in. She pulled her dress over her head with easy, matter-of-fact movements. Often on a Sunday afternoon they lay down like this on top of the bed, and she always took off her dress so it wouldn't get creased.

She lay down beside him, not touching him, on her back with her hands behind her head. They could hear the twins' mother on the other side of the wall washing dishes; she had the radio on.

On the third floor, one of Mademoiselle Strieb's pupils was endlessly repeating the same passage on the piano— the one they'd heard played by every beginner for years. A long way away, perhaps on rue du Pas-de-la-Mule, a pneumatic drill was breaking up the street.

They lay motionless, silent, as though trying to steep themselves in each other's thoughts. Bernard, at least, was thinking only about his wife and what she had told him about her morning. He was stirred by the discovery that they had been unhappy together, without knowing it, for more or less identical reasons.

"You know, Nelly . . ."

They were not looking at each other. Each of them was staring at the ceiling, where two flies were silently chasing each other.

"What do I know?"

"To come right down to it, I've always been jealous."

"I know. At Epinal you never liked introducing your friends to me."

"I didn't have any close friends. . . . Not before, either. . . . Or afterward . . ."

It was like a duet, with the voices hesitant. First one and then the other ventured a little phrase, and gradually the themes began to intermingle.

"One evening, when a boy asked me to dance . . ."

"I'm talking of before that . . ."

"Before you knew me?"

"Yes."

"You were in love with another woman?"

"I wasn't in love with anybody, but I was already jealous. It's hard to explain. Just now, when you went down to telephone, I remembered something from when I was little, and I said to myself I'd tell you about it.

"I was five or six years old. Not quite six, because I was still at the nursery school. I used to spend hours in the courtyard, or under the arches around Place des Vosges. Mother kept an eye on me, but from quite a distance.

"I'd discovered a little girl, younger than I was, and she was left alone in the square all day. I don't know if she had a father. Her mother was Italian and went out to work in the district. Even to us, who were poor people, she seemed very poor.

"The girl's name was Rita. . . . I had trouble remembering her name, although for quite a long time she filled an important place in my life."

"You loved her?" asked Nelly, very touched.

"Wait! Let me try to tell the real truth. . . . I wasn't in love with her, but in my mind she was my wife, because she was the most defenseless and submissive creature I'd been able to find. She had skinny legs, and her face looked brown with ingrained dirt. I remember her eyes: they were big, brown, and shining, with a fixed stare that was fascinating."

"What did you do together?"

"At the far end of the courtyard, near what had once been the stables, a door led into a little room with no window, where my mother kept her brooms and pails. I used to take Rita there."

"Shutting the door?"

"Yes."

"You stayed in there in the dark?"

"Yes. And I was afraid of the dark."

"What did you play?"

"We didn't play. She was my wife—or my slave; I forget which. I probably didn't know which even then. In that broom closet we were by ourselves, and I felt I was the master."

"Did you ever kiss her?"

"I never even thought of it. I didn't hit her either. I used to tell her to sit down with her back to the wall, and I'd sit there beside her."

"Wasn't she frightened?"

"That idea never occurred to me. I don't think so. When I heard Mother calling me in, I'd go out, and shut the door behind me."

"Leaving her alone?"

"Yes . . . One day, that led to a scene. Her mother was looking everywhere for her; she came into our courtyard, calling 'Rita! . . . Rita!' and some words in Italian. . . . My mother was just assuring her that she hadn't seen her little girl all day, when they heard a tiny voice, which seemed to come from a long distance; it sounded stifled. They found Rita finally, and her mother accused mine of having shut her in to get rid of her while I ate. . . ."

"Didn't you say it wasn't true?"

"I wonder. I don't remember how it ended. I only wanted to explain to you what I'm trying to explain to myself. I often think about it. . . ."

"About being jealous?"

"About you . . . About me . . . I love you and I'm jealous. . . . Don't interrupt. . . . That's the truth, and it's not as nice as I'd like it to be. . . . Even if I didn't love you and you were my wife, I'd be jealous, and it would make me miserable. . . . Can you understand that?"

"Maybe. Have you often been miserable over me?"

"Off and on . . . It comes, and then it goes and I'm perfectly happy. . . . I felt like saying 'madly happy,' because there are days when I could shout for joy when I see you getting off the bus. . . . Ever since I was fourteen I wanted to get married, to have a wife of my own and a little world where I would be . . ."

He hesitated.

"As you see, it's nothing to be proud of. . . . A world in which I'd be the center, where I'd be the master . . . Not so much to give orders, as to feel I was the strongest . . . I imagined a wife who would need me, who would have nothing in the world, one I would have to protect and make happy. . . ."

"You've made me happy. . . ."

He shook his head; he was still lying flat on his back, and Nelly had laid a timid hand on his hip. She did not move again, and there were long pauses during which the life outside came more noisily through the window, where the curtains were billowing gently.

"What I've been saying isn't exactly what I mean, even so. . . . It's more complicated, perhaps too complicated for me. . . . I admired my father tremendously, and you'll never guess why. . . ."

"I bet it was because of the horses."

"When I was very small, yes, but that didn't last long. What seemed marvelous to me later on was the way Father set out alone with his wagon into the scary world of Paris. . . . My life had narrow frontiers; even rue Saint-Antoine seemed foreign and dangerous to me. But Father went everywhere, loading heavy things in a railroad station near whistling engines, driving among streetcars, buses, and taxis. . . . In my eyes it was as extraordinary as the Red Indians on the warpath in a picture book."

"Did you plan, when you grew up, to . . ."

"No . . . I don't think so. . . . Anyhow, he died about that time. What I really admired . . ."

He broke off to laugh at himself.

"This is the first time I've ever thought out loud in front of anyone, and now you see how difficult it is. . . . As a matter of fact, I have whole days to myself to think things out. But do I? . . .

"The real reason I admired my father was that he didn't need anybody. He could sit down in the evening in front of our door, all alone. He didn't read the paper, he didn't listen to the radio. He sat there, letting his pipe go out, staring into space with an air of contentment. . . ."

"You couldn't have lived alone, could you?"

"No. I always knew I needed a wife."

"Is that why you married me?" she teased him.

"I loved you. But if I hadn't met you, I'd have got married just the same."

"And you'd have been jealous?"

"I'm almost sure I would. But it wouldn't have hurt me so much . . ."

"Do you think about it every day?"

"No. But as soon as you're not here, I feel uneasy, anxious."

"Me, too. Do you remember, when they raised your pension, I suggested, timidly, that I might stop working? I didn't dare insist. I was afraid you'd think I was lazy."

"I hesitated," he admitted. "I even spoke to Dr. Aubonne. . . ."

"Why to him?"

"Because it was a great responsibility to take. I didn't want to think only of myself."

"What did he say?"

"That for both our sakes, it was better for us each to have a separate job."

"Would you like me to leave Delangle & Abouet? . . . Shall I?"

"No . . ."

"Why not?"

"Because you need an outlet for your energy, and here you wouldn't have enough. . . ."

"In that case . . ."

"Wait! I need to be able to say to myself . . ."

He didn't finish his sentence at once; he waited for his confession to be sincere, completely truthful, but felt, dejectedly, that he wouldn't manage it.

"What do you need to be able to say to yourself?"

"I live my life at second hand, in a way. . . . You go out. . . . You come home. . . . You see people, streets, things happening. . . . When you get home you're soaked in it all. . . . I say to myself it's partly thanks to me, because I don't condemn you to play the nurse from morning to night. . . . Come to think of it, I'm very selfish."

"You, selfish?"

"Yes. It's no use arguing. . . . I think so much about myself, about us, that I'm finally getting to know myself well. The reason I put up such resistance to Aubonne, and even more to Pellet, who's much cleverer, is that I was determined they wouldn't discover the truth. They were always trying to make me say I had worries. . . ."

There was a pause, rather strained, because he had referred indirectly to an apartment on the second floor, a door he had never opened, a white china knob he had never touched. He avoided any more direct allusion to Mazeron, but even so it was as though the man had suddenly appeared.

"I don't know why I felt wretched from the very first day, from the moment I knew he would be coming to live in this house. . . . I didn't know then that you'd be having to see him. . . . The idea that another cripple . . ."

Silence again, while Nelly held her breath.

"That wasn't what brought on my dizziness. Really it wasn't. I'd had attacks of that already. . . . It was just that I began to have them more often, and more violently, every time you went in to see him or I thought of the two of you. . . ."

"The two of us?"

"Forgive me. . . . That's how it was in my mind. . . ."

"You really imagined . . ."

"Sometimes I did, sometimes I didn't. . . . It doesn't

88

matter. . . . The mere fact of your taking even the slightest interest in anyone else . . . And even more if it's someone who needs help, like me, someone who's lonely and unhappy. . . ."

"He isn't unhappy."

"Ah!"

"On the contrary. I'm pretty sure he's having a blissful love affair with the nurse, who brings him flowers and little treats every day. . . . I think she poses for him."

"In the nude?"

"Well, there are nudes on the walls, drawings that look like her. . . . I've only passed her on the stairs twice, but . . ."

"He hasn't asked you to pose for him?"

"Never."

"You see the way I am! A word, a mental picture, and off I go. . . . If you went out right now, I'd begin imagining all kinds of things again. . . . I know it's absurd, hateful. . . . I love you. . . . I declare that all I want is your happiness. . . . And then, at the idea that you might be interested in another man, that you might feel tempted . . ."

"Don't!"

"It's happened to me, after all, and I love you just as much. . . . "

"Often?"

"Three times . . . Two real times, and another that doesn't really count."

"Long ago?"

"The first was when I was still working at the garage. . . . Heaven only knows, you and I were passionately in love, and we used to make love . . . Well, in spite of that, I felt the need to go to bed with another woman. . . ."

"Who was she?"

"I don't know her name, and I'm sure I wouldn't recognize her. I was working the gas pump, out by the sidewalk. It was very hot. You and I had had lunch together at a cheap little restaurant, and I'd had several glasses of wine, just like today. It wasn't forbidden to me in those days. Remember? Sometimes we both drank just a little too much, on purpose, and it would make me laugh to see how your eyes lit up. . . ."

"And it was with this other woman . . ."

"She was walking up and down outside the hotel almost next door to the garage. . . . She had big breasts. Yours were very small. All of a sudden I wanted to hold big breasts in my hands. . . . I pretended to be going for a quick drink, left the garage for a few minutes, and followed her into the hotel. . . ."

"Did you enjoy it?"

"I forget. . . . But I remember I was in terror for several weeks, thinking I might have caught an infection and given it to you. . . . And *I'm* the one who gets sick with jealousy!"

"And the other two?"

"Am I upsetting you?"

"No. I'd rather know everything, really everything."

"The second was during the war, in a village in Alsace where we were quartered. The civilians hadn't all been evacuated yet. The captain was billeted in a private house, and I sometimes had to take letters to him.

"His landlady was still young, very blond, with blue eyes, and she had two children, even blonder. Her husband was in the army somewhere in the Ardennes. . . .

"One morning, when I had a message for the captain, no one came to the front door, so I went in. I knocked at all the doors, and finally I opened one and found this woman in the room, making her bed."

"You took her, just like that?"

"More or less . . . She didn't speak French. I didn't speak or understand German. . . . I was carrying a fat yellow envelope, and I don't know why, but both of us suddenly burst out laughing. . . .

"A few seconds later we were on the bed; and the whole time it lasted I was looking at a photograph in front of my nose, with her as a bride and her husband in a suit that was too tight for him. . . .

"Probably he came back from the war and they had some more children. . . . You understand?"

"And the third?"

"That was by way of being an act of charity. . . . Not on my part . . . I was still in the château that was turned into a field hospital, where I was taken first and had the luck to meet Aubonne. I was in a bad way. . . . I wasn't allowed up, because I was still running a temperature. . . .

"There were voluntary nurses looking after us, and I gave them a lot of trouble, being restless at night and trying to tear off the dressings when I was delirious. . . ."

She pressed a little closer to his side.

"Go on."

"It's silly. I feel one shouldn't talk about such things to a woman, not even to one's wife. . . ."

"Well, now that you've begun . . ."

"They were giving me injections to calm me down, first in the left thigh, then in the right. One evening when I was tossing, and the other fellows had gone to sleep . . ."

"How many were there in the room?"

"Six or seven, depending on the size of the room and the position of the windows . . . The night nurse gave me a shot. . . . Just then, while I was uncovered, I had an erection. . . . It wasn't because of her, or of anything I was thinking about. It was kind of mechanical, and I blushed.

"She sat down by the bed, as usual, waiting for the shot to work; but I was still fidgety. So she slipped her hand gently under the sheet and began to caress me, looking at me with an expression that was half amused and half pitying. . . .

"I don't think I ever felt so embarrassed in all my life. But I never felt such subtle pleasure, either. I mean the physical sensation, you understand. My arms were hurting, the drug was beginning to work, and it all fitted in with . . ."

"How old was she?"

"Twenty-three or twenty-four."

"Did you see her again?"

"In that hospital, yes, in the two weeks I was still there . . ."

"Did she do it again?"

"No."

"You didn't ask her to?"

"No."

"She wasn't embarrassed with you?"

"Well, there was the war. . . . She may have expected me to die, as so many others were doing. . . . She must be married now, and have children. . . ."

"I wonder whether she remembers."

"Do you remember?" he asked in a different tone.

"Remember what?"

"You know what I mean. . . . Before me . . ."

"I used to think so little of it. . . . You forget the kind of home I had, and how, when I was still tiny, I'd seen my mother . . ."

"Hush!"

"You asked me. . . ."

Finally he brought out a question he had never ventured to ask her before.

"Soldiers?"

"There were some soldiers."

"Ones I knew?"

"I don't think so. I hardly knew them. . . ."

"Boys from the town, too?"

"Yes."

"Where did it happen?"

She, who had just been questioning him, was answering reluctantly, sadly.

"Have you forgotten? In the woods? By the stream?"

"Yes, and sometimes on a bench in the park . . . Only once did I go to a proper room and undress. I felt ashamed. . . . Why did you want to know?"

"So as to stop thinking about it."

"What do you mean?"

"That if I know exactly what happened, and what's happening, I'll stop wondering. But I have to be sure. . . ."

"You're jealous of before, too?"

"I'm jealous of everything, even of your father!"

She stiffened.

"My father never tried to . . ."

"It doesn't need that. . . . He was living with you, he had rights over you. . . .

"And afterward, when I was called up?"

She shook her head. The piano was playing more quickly, a more difficult piece; Mademoiselle Strieb had a different pupil now.

Next door the radio had been turned off. It was replaced by a monotonous murmur of women's voices. This was the day Madame Rougin's sister-in-law always came to see her, and they chattered on all afternoon.

"Never?"

"Never, Bernard, I swear to you."

"You were never tempted to, even once?"

"I was far from thinking about it! At night I used to dream you were dead or wounded, that you were calling me, and I'd wake up with a start. . . ."

"No men made love to you?"

"Made love to me—no. A few tried, the way they always do. . . . Like you with the Alsatian woman," she added with a short laugh.

"The Alsatian woman didn't push me away, although it was happening next to her husband's picture. We could hear her children playing in the street. . . ."

"Well, I did."

"Why?"

"I really don't know. . . . If you don't understand, I can't explain. If you were a woman . . ."

"And nowadays, at work?"

"What?"

"The salesmen."

"Now and then a new one asks me to lunch, or to go out with him in the evening."

"What do you say?"

"I say no."

"You don't tell them you're married?"

"It's not necessary. They understand at once."

"And Jean-Paul?"

It was the first time he had referred to the assistant manager like that.

"Him? He's too busy with his modernization plans to bother about any of us. All that interests him is to show old Delangle and, still more, his own father that he can run the business better than they can."

"And . . ."

"And what? The butcher? The grocer, poor Monsieur Bourre? Who else?"

She had returned to a playful tone that was infectious. Life and their problems seemed easy again.

"I've told you more than you've told me," Bernard growled in feigned annoyance.

"That shows you had more to confess."

Having thus reverted to the past, his thoughts now took a fresh turn.

"What are you laughing at?" she asked.

"At us. Or at myself . . . At what happened the month after we were married."

They used to walk a lot, all over Paris, though they had their favorite districts. It was not unusual for them to walk up to Sacré Coeur and come down again via Pigalle, where, having no money in their pockets, they sated themselves with the outside glitter of night life.

At other times they chose the Grands Boulevards, which had not yet surrendered their glamour to the Champs-Elysées, especially between the Opéra and the Madeleine. They knew all the shop windows there, and would linger in front of them with wondering eyes.

"When we're rich . . ."

For them, as for all humble people, the word "rich" carried a different meaning from the dictionary one. It meant having a little money left over after paying the rent, buying food and essential clothing, and settling the gas and electricity bills.

"When we're rich . . ."

They were fond of the quays along the Seine, too— sometimes following them all the way to Charenton—and the narrow streets in the Latin Quarter.

"The little restaurant . . ." he said softly, to put her on the track.

A real bistro, with a red-painted front, a zinc-topped bar, paper tablecloths, and a door at the back leading into the kitchen, where a fat man was busy at the stove.

"Come! I bet they'll have *andouillette.* . . ."

They both liked *andouillette.* They sat down at a table near the door. It was eight o'clock in the evening, and they were surprised to see no one else there. Bernard thought everyone had gone already; he had no idea that they had not yet arrived, and wouldn't begin to until eight-thirty or nine.

Not until the waiter offered him a huge menu printed on paper as thick as cartridge paper did he understand. The least of the hors d'oeuvres cost as much as an entire meal in the restaurants he was accustomed to, and his whole week's wages would scarcely have paid for two dinners.

Nelly, who hadn't seen the menu, wondered why he was sitting there in silence, like a stuck pig, while the waiter watched them quizzically.

Bernard hesitated, not knowing how to get out of it.

"I think . . . er . . . we'll come back later."

As time went by it had become an amusing memory.

"Do you remember the spaniel?"

On the Champs-Elysées there was a pet shop, up at the top, on the right. The window was full of dogs of all kinds, cats, parrots. One of the little cages held a spaniel bitch with her three puppies, and Nelly couldn't tear her eyes away from them.

"Bernard, let's buy a dog."

She had lost her heart to one of the puppies, the one with the pinkest tip to its nose.

"He'd be company for me when I'm home alone all day."

In those days she had been the one who stayed at home waiting.

"A good thing we didn't buy him! What would I have done with him when you went away, and how would we have fed him during the war?"

Silence again. They had come still closer together, touching each other from head to foot.

"I have an idea," she said.

"What is it?"

"Why don't we buy a dog now? It would be your dog."

"No! I'd rather be alone, even if at times I . . ."

"Shh!"

He stopped. She felt hot beside him, and her breathing was growing quicker.

"Bernard . . ."

"Yes?"

"Would you like to?"

At five o'clock the table had still not been cleared and the bottle of wine was still there—in a paler light, because the sun had moved around to another window and was no longer touching it.

"How do you feel?" she whispered in his ear.

"Fine. Aching a little . . ."

"Me, I feel as though I'd just recovered from flu. . . ."

They had stood leaning on the window rail, looking out, and then Nelly had gone to tidy up. A bus full of tourists drove past; there would be a string of them for the next two months.

In a few days, on July 14, there would be dancing in Place des Vosges, with the sound of exploding rockets and the colored stars of fireworks raining down beyond the nearby roofs.

Next door, the twins were squabbling not only with their

97

mother but also with their aunt, who had an even more piercing voice.

At twenty minutes past six he saw the bus on which his wife usually came home, and it was strange to hear her moving about behind him.

Soon—perhaps before dinner, but more likely afterward, while they sat in their respective chairs watching the dusk fall—he must speak to her again.

He had just come to a decision.

Chapter Six

THE JULY 14 FESTIVITIES were over. They had roamed together beneath the fairy lights, keeping back in the shadow to avoid the thick of the crowd. A military band played on the bandstand in Place des Vosges, and a not very good jazz band on each of the platforms outside the two cafés, which had extended their terraces. Among the host of people, the eye was quick to single out faces seen every day on neighborhood streets and in the shops.

Beer and wine stood on the café tables. Some couples were dancing, as though the music had been composed especially for them; watching, one might have made a game out of guessing their history.

At midnight children were still scampering around underfoot. At the corner of rue de Birague a little girl, like the Rita of thirty-seven or thirty-eight years ago, was sobbing bitterly because she had lost her mother.

About one o'clock, a storm burst, sending people running helter-skelter. The rain fell so hard that some men took their jackets off and used them to protect their own heads or their companions'. After a few seconds, the women's thin dresses were clinging to their bodies so closely that some of them might have been naked.

Since then the weather had remained uncertain, the sky a heavy gray most of the time, and the air muggy. Every day, toward evening, there was a shower, accompanied by the rumble of distant thunder.

Bernard couldn't decide whether what he had done was right or wrong. He had acted as he thought best. Yet he wondered whether, with certain words, certain phrases, he had not defined too clearly what until then had remained vague and thus had provided food for his nightmares.

Not to mention the fact that he no longer had to carry their weight unaided. The thoughts he had described so lightly had not vanished into thin air afterward, but remained with them, between them; they had established themselves, invisibly, in the privacy of the apartment.

Bernard and Nelly talked to each other in their usual way, spoke the same words, made the same gestures. He still stood at the window, waving his arm when she waved her hand to him before getting into her bus. When she came home, she found lunch or dinner ready, the table set, and the door always open before she reached the landing.

They hadn't made the Grand Tour again, but they had taken an evening stroll around the square, pausing outside the antique shop. They knew everything in the window, so they could see at a glance if any item was missing.

They often smiled at each other affectionately, perhaps more affectionately than ever before in their lives; but with the faintest touch of embarrassment, of bashfulness, as though each of them had done something that needed forgiveness.

There was no bitterness between them—far from it. Bernard felt he had never loved Nelly so dearly, while she seemed to cling to him more, sometimes almost with bated breath.

He could not have said for certain whether the afternoon when she had not gone back to the office had caused the almost imperceptible change, or whether it had been their conversation that evening at the open window. Despite the serious things they had said to each other, the afternoon had left with him a feeling of lightness, a certain rippling sprightliness.

They had lain on the bed, leaving long pauses between their sentences, and though they had seemed to be playing with dangerous ideas, it had remained a game, and they had been left with amusing memories before making love, gently, smiling as though appeased.

Afterward they had lain a long time without moving, listening to their breathing and the beating of their hearts, which mingled with more distant sounds.

Was it then that he had made a mistake, had a bad idea? Or had it all come out of the general events of that day, beginning with the scene at breakfast, then the wine he had drunk at lunch, the secrets he had insisted on telling her?

He could not decide, and his dizzy spells came more and more frequently. Even in the quiet of the apartment, terror would seize him without warning, and the walls, the furniture, the familiar possessions would seem to lose their comforting solidity. At such times he kept away from the open windows; he was afraid he might fall out.

What he needed was to be able to stop thinking, to turn a knob and cut off the current, as you do with a radio. Unfortunately, that wasn't possible. Aubonne, who must be back from Portugal by now, would not be coming to see him for another two or three weeks. Anyway, how could he help? He would simply urge him again to go away, without realizing that away from his familiar surroundings he would feel more lost than ever. He might prescribe some new tranquilizer, although Bernard was almost frighteningly tranquil.

The fact was, his problem no longer came within the sphere of medicine. He was not ill.

Perhaps, too, he had been unwise to finish the bottle of wine that evening. It had made no difference, though, because his mind was made up before he went to lean on the window rail while Nelly tidied the room.

It was while lying beside her on the bed, at his happiest and most relaxed, that he had thought of it. All that he had said before they made love had been true. He had been as sincere as possible. His jealousy dated from before Nelly's time. It was a kind of blemish in his character, and, since he knew this, had openly admitted it, he no longer had the right to make another person miserable with it.

He had confessed that his jealousy of Mazeron was all the more excruciating because Mazeron was a cripple, too. He might have added, carrying the thing to its conclusion, that Mazeron was a young man, only twenty-eight, that he still had both his hands and that, as Nelly herself had admitted, he was cheerful and carefree.

"You must let me talk right on, without objecting or interrupting me. . . ."

Dusk was blurring their features, making it impossible to read any expression on their faces. There were lights across the street already, figures moving around in the rooms; the man with the bad heart was reading his newspaper, turning a page from time to time.

"Tomorrow you must tell Gisèle that I didn't know what you were going to say to her this morning. . . ."

"Bernard! Please . . ."

"Wait! I want to do this properly. I mean what I say. . . . I've been thinking it over. . . ."

"You want . . ."

"I want everything to be as it was before. . . . Tell Gisèle you spoke to me about it, that I disagreed, that I don't care a damn what the neighbors think. . . . I can't bear the idea that a boy who's in no way responsible has to suffer because of my jealousy. . . ."

"But what's the point?"

"Let's say I'm doing my duty to other people, and to myself. . . . Otherwise, I'd be ashamed to know you were crossing that landing four times a day with your head turned away. . . . And ashamed of what he'd think when he heard you. . . . You understand?"

"I think I'm beginning to."

"It's not so much for his sake or yours. It's for my own."

"You won't be miserable?"

"No."

"You won't start imagining things again?"

"I'll try not to."

"And if you can't help it?"

"It'll make no difference. I told you, I imagine things anyhow. I've been getting ideas about your boss too. . . . The same with the bus conductor, and any other man you meet. . . ."

"My poor Bernard . . ."

He felt strong. He was determined to be strong. It was she who raised objections.

"Gisèle will think we quarreled, that I was the one who insisted that . . ."

"It's not Gisèle who matters. It's us."

"Particularly since I didn't go back to the office this afternoon."

"If I were to behave differently, there'd be no point in having talked to you the way I have."

"It did you good?"

"I think so. . . . I love you, little Nelly. . . . You know, there are thousands and thousands of buildings all around us, hundreds of thousands of apartments like ours, with married couples enjoying the cool evening at the window. . . . They're all trying to be happy. . . . I'm sure they're all doing their best. And they're all trying not to hurt each other. . . . Did I hurt you much?"

"I'd rather know. . . . Now that you've told me everything, it seems to me . . ."

"It seems to you what?"

"I'm not sure. . . . It seems to me I'll be less worried, especially if you have fewer dizzy spells. From what you say, that would mean you weren't tormenting yourself so much."

"You know, one mustn't make a tragedy of things. . . . When I find myself looking too much on the dark side, I think of a funeral. The whole family is heartbroken, in floods of tears . . . thinking life will never be the same again. . . . And then somebody—often the widow, or a sister-in-law—goes to the sideboard and brings out the decanter of liqueur and the set of little glasses. . . . Nobody feels like drinking, but everyone takes a sip, out of politeness. Once the glasses are empty, they're automatically refilled; and soon somebody begins telling funny stories. . . ."

"Is that what you'd do if I died?"

"I couldn't go on living without you."

"Then what's the point of your story?"

"That I don't spend my days moping. . . . I listen to the

radio, I do the cooking, I potter, I whistle, and now and then I laugh out loud at something I remember. . . . I've been telling you about the bad moments, without mentioning the good ones. . . . If I added them up, there'd probably be more good ones."

"So you aren't unhappy?"

"No! It's the same with noise. Every time I hear a door bang, my first reaction is anger, because the noise hurts my ears. And the twins make the whole place shake whenever they go in or out. In the morning, the diesel trucks can be heard from as far away as Boulevard du Temple. I grumble. I growl. But it never occurs to me to shut the window, and if there was a sudden silence, I'd feel quite lost. Probably during the vacation I'll even miss the children getting out of school."

"You're a strange man. I wonder . . ."

"Go on."

"I'm afraid of hurting you again. . . . I wonder if you'd have been the same without your injury. . . ."

"We'd probably have mixed more with other people. We'd have shared in their lives. . . . You remember when we were exploring Paris? We really were part of the crowd. . . . Instead of that now, I stay in my corner, watching and listening. . . . It comes to the same thing, really, except that I need you even more. . . ."

Later, when she was undressing, she murmured, with a puzzled frown: "You really think I should?"

"Tomorrow morning you must speak to Gisèle, without going into a long explanation—as though it were quite simple and natural."

Next day, when she came home for lunch, he asked: "Well?"

"It's done."

"What did she say?"

"That it was what she'd have expected of you and that you were a sweetie."

"Didn't she have any message for him?"

"Not this morning."

Why had he seemed to see something a little unnatural in her manner? She looked at him with eyes that were too cloudless, as though wanting him to see she was keeping nothing back.

"I had to give the date for my vacation. It's the personnel manager who takes care of that."

Didn't that mean "So I didn't need to go to Monsieur Jean-Paul's office"?

"I asked for August 15, just as we decided. It isn't worth taking the first half of August, since we're not going away, and it doesn't matter much to us if it rains or gets cool."

"Would you rather we went away?"

"No. I enjoy Paris, particularly when the streets are nearly empty. If you feel well, we'll go for long walks."

Her smile was so radiant he wondered if it was forced. It was his own fault; he realized that. She knew now that the slightest lapse, the most casual remark, might evoke some idea that would plunge him back into his evil thoughts and cause him physical suffering. She was so anxious to seem natural that now she wasn't.

"You're sure it's the nurse who posed for the drawings?"

"I think so, but I'm not positive. They're charcoal, on big sheets of paper, fastened to the wall with drawing pins. Some of them don't show the face; in others it's only a vague profile."

"Why did you tell me it was the nurse?"

"Because no other women visit him."

"How do you know?"

"His sister tells me no one visits him. Before his illness, he lived in Lyon—that's where they come from—and worked on a newspaper. He knows hardly anybody in Paris."

It had all begun again! With the additional factor that now he was drinking half a bottle of wine with every meal. Even that had sprung from good intentions. The day of his closest intimacy with Nelly, he had drunk several glasses of wine without realizing it, first at lunch and then in the evening, when he'd finished the bottle. He continued to, owing to a kind of superstition, thinking it might produce the same effect every time, give them that feeling of lightness he now found unbelievable.

What happened was just the opposite. He didn't get drunk, or drink enough to feel muddled. His thoughts were emphasized, as it were, by the wine, and the least of them would suddenly take on alarming importance.

The day after the pretended visit to the dentist, he had watched for the bus as usual, and looked at once at his wife's hands. She was not carrying a package. They had exchanged their usual signals, and immediately afterward he had gone to open the front door.

He'd promised himself not to listen, but the temptation was too strong. The footsteps had stopped on the second floor. He thought he sensed hesitation. Then Nelly had knocked on the door—not loudly and not for long—and turned the knob.

He'd wondered in the past whether she shut the door behind her. She didn't. But she must have gone fairly far in, because when he leaned over the banister he could not hear voices.

It took less than two minutes. She closed the door, hurried upstairs, ran into the living room, and kissed him. It was very hot, since it hadn't rained that day, and she smelled of sweat.

"You haven't done any work?"

She was looking at the white lampshades lined up on the shelf, and at the table set for lunch.

"You had something for him?"

"No."

"Not even a letter?"

"Not even that! I suspect she gave me a message on purpose, to pay me back for what I said to her yesterday. I just had to tell him that everything was settled, that two of his drawings—he'd know which—had been accepted."

"Why didn't he come and open the door?"

"He never does. The hall's too narrow for him to turn his wheelchair."

"Can't he walk at all?"

"Only with two canes."

"Was he standing up?"

"No. Sitting in his armchair."

"What was he doing?"

"Reading the newspaper. He reads a lot of newspapers and magazines, because of his work."

"What did he say?"

"Just thanked me."

"Was that all?"

"He also said that if he felt up to working this evening he'd have more drawings ready to take to his sister tomorrow morning."

"So she's the one who runs around to the newspapers, instead of him?"

"How could he do it?"

Was she thinking, as he was, that he ought not to question her like that?

"This may be a silly idea," she said softly, "but I wonder

whether, next time there's a package or a message for him, it wouldn't be better for *you* to take it. It might help you to understand; you'd see there can't be anything between us."

Why had she added, "He's still just a boy"?

Her voice as she said that had a protective sound that reminded him of the nurse at the château hospital. He had been a boy himself in those days. She was young, but he was even younger, and lying there in bed he'd looked as helpless as a little child.

Indeed, she had treated him rather like a child—not quite like a man, anyway.

There was nothing in common between Nelly and that girl, whose name he didn't even know. Or between his wife and the Alsatian woman.

Yes, there was though! One thing! All three of them were women. And the husband in the badly cut black suit, whose photo he had seen by the bed, was a man like himself.

Was the man happy, now? Had he ever wondered what might have gone on while he was at the front? No doubt he'd had his little affairs, like all soldiers. All of them were convinced—Bernard as much as any—that, in the meantime, their wives were behaving virtuously!

Why? It began to stab at his mind. Everything became a cause of uneasiness—Nelly's smiles as much as her pouts and fits of absentmindedness, her moments of gaiety as much as the times when she looked worried.

"A penny for your thoughts!"

If she jumped, he inferred that she had been far away, that she had given him the slip yet again. If she produced some commonplace reply at once, he wondered if she'd prepared it beforehand.

Surely it was improbable, almost impossible, that she

had remained faithful to him all along, even when he was far away and she wasn't sure he would come back, even when he was lying helpless in bed.

Hadn't she admitted that for a girl with her upbringing, the sexual act had no importance? She'd submitted to it on the benches in the park in Epinal. And she and he had made love in places where, perhaps, she'd lain on the grass with other men, soldiers like himself or civilians.

Hadn't she sounded rather proud—even though she'd said she was ashamed—when she announced that once, at least, she'd gone to a proper room and been able to undress?

When his thoughts took that turn, it made his fingers ache, as though they were still there, as though he were digging his nails into the palms of his hands. Afterward, feeling sick, he would ask himself when all this had begun.

After all, he'd been living with her for twenty years, and he hadn't always tortured himself like this. He was jealous, of course, as he had good reason to believe most men were. Was it because he felt he was growing old, while his wife seemed to get younger and younger?

Or were the doctors wrong in thinking there was nothing seriously wrong with his health?

The various associations for disabled ex-servicemen sent him their bulletins regularly, but most of the time he merely glanced at the page dealing with pensions. Now and then, however, he happened to read an article; and he now remembered one that had not impressed him much at the time. It was about men who, after losing limbs, had put up with their condition bravely for years, and then, at the age of forty-five up to fifty, had suddenly become neurasthenic.

It was strange. When they were still young and full of

life, and must have felt their loss most keenly, they had borne it almost gaily. Then, as they grew older, they seemed to realize what they had missed, developed a grudge against society, and began to take it out on their nearest and dearest.

Some of them went as far as suicide, and it was almost always planned far ahead, down to the smallest detail, as though it was the inevitable outcome of a long incubation period.

Just recently, in the Batignolles district, a man who had suffered serious head injuries had shot his neighbor dead with a rifle because the man persisted in turning his radio on full blast.

And wasn't he himself beginning to dislike the twins because they banged doors and had shrill voices?

That didn't explain why his jealousy was becoming an obsession—perhaps made worse because it was a point of honor not to show it. He had said enough on the subject, probably too much. Poor Nelly didn't know what to do next; whatever she did he found reason to be suspicious of it an hour or so later.

Why had she suggested he go see Pierre Mazeron? Hadn't it been in the hope that they'd strike up a friendship?

There are so many couples who are not self-sufficient; instead, they feel the need to get together with others in the evening. They couldn't invite Mazeron to their apartment because of the stairs, but they could go to his. Being the eldest, Bernard would probably be expected to talk most. And Nelly and Mazeron would exchange conspiratorial glances behind his back.

Damn it all, that happens, too! There was no reason it shouldn't happen to him, as it did to so many others, even those with two hands. Perhaps it had been like that for a long time, not with Mazeron, but with other men.

There had been a time, a few years ago, when an old acquaintance of Bernard's, whom he had met again accidentally in the district, used to come and see them, bringing his wife. They were living then on Boulevard Beaumarchais; later, they moved away to Limoges.

Bernard and he had worked together at the garage. His name was Lesueur, but everyone called him Fred. Every evening, a girl—not always the same one—was waiting for him when he left work. He not only changed girls often, but also was apt to have three or four at the same time. His co-workers used to joke about him and call him "the stallion."

It was true that he was a powerfully built, full-blooded man, seemed very conscious of his virility, and often referred to his attributes in coarse language. He would even exhibit them, out of boastfulness or as a challenge.

Wasn't it a male like that of whom Nelly was dreaming when she began to toss around at night? In the early days, in Epinal, she, too, had shocked him by using words he would not have dared utter in front of her; and even now, sometimes, when they were making love, she would mutter them through clenched teeth, like an incantation.

Aside from working hours, she never left the house without him except when it was she who had to do the shopping, but . . .

One morning, yielding to a ridiculous temptation, he took the bus to rue d'Aboukir. It was a long time since he had been near Place des Victoires, or seen the four tall windows on the second floor of Delangle & Abouet's premises.

Slinking along close to the wall, afraid of being seen, he

went into a bistro on rue des Petits-Pères, from which he could see the building across the square.

He was ashamed of himself, because he didn't know what he had come to look for. Musing about this, he forgot to give his order, and the blue-aproned waiter stared at him and then winked at an old taxi driver leaning against the bar.

"A glass of wine," he said, without pausing to think.

On the second floor of the building he could see the lights hanging from the ceiling, rows of shelves, women in gray smocks going back and forth in a strange light. He didn't recognize Nelly, who must be among them, because he was too far away—though not so far that he didn't notice a dark-haired man, who appeared now and then.

She was at home over there, too, talking and working, perhaps humming while she worked. People unknown to him were almost as important a part of her life as he was; other voices and faces were as familiar to her as his.

He wished he could hide inside the room, to watch her movements and the expressions on her face, in order to discover what she was like when he was not there.

Whenever he asked her what had happened at work, she always replied, with a shrug: "Nothing interesting."

Nothing interesting to him, because he didn't belong to that world, and it would have taken too long to explain everything to him.

That "nothing interesting" went on for eight hours a day. When she got home it wasn't as though she had come out of seclusion. She'd come out of life, out of a particular life, one that was more eventful and enthralling than the life she led at home.

What did he give her in life? They were husband and wife, well and good. They made love. Even so, it was she who had to take the initiative in certain things that are usually the man's prerogative.

Surely it must have been hard for her to overcome her repugnance at the sight of his two shapeless stumps marked by the prosthesis, which were removed at night, especially when she had to powder or rub them with ointment.

Apart from that—even if, physically speaking, he satisfied her? He cooked the meals, but she could have eaten better at any little restaurant. It was she who got up at six in the morning to do the housework, give him his bath, and help him into his prosthesis.

. . . The stroll around Place des Vosges, haunted, for the last few months, by the fear of seeing him suddenly overcome by dizziness. More and more frequently, he walked with slow, faltering steps, like an invalid.

. . . The same old arches overhead, and the everlasting antique shop with its window, the contents of which they always inspected, with the same gravity.

. . . The Grand Tour, at rare intervals. Or the movies on Boulevard du Temple, which exasperated Bernard if the film was too noisy. That wasn't his fault; some noises caused him physical suffering. Once, they had been obliged to leave.

Was that a life for a young woman?

He did not consider himself a hero. He had done nothing remarkable, and it was by accident, with no thought of danger, that he had stumbled on that mine. He had been cared for, transferred from one hospital to another, and laws had been passed later on for the rehabilitation of soldiers in his circumstances.

He had refused rehabilitation, being content to go on painting his lampshades. He was entitled to. They paid him a pension, and he did what he wanted with it.

He had never been bitter—on the whole, he felt his position was rather enviable.

Why was he now beginning to get irritable when he was jostled in the street by someone who hadn't noticed his hooks?

Nelly would soon be coming out. A bell rang, he knew, on each of the four floors of offices and salesrooms. She would hurry to take off her smock, pick up her bag, put on a little powder and lipstick.

He didn't wait till that moment; he took a taxi, to get home before her, and felt angry with himself for the unnecessary expense, for the whole silly escapade.

He had seen nothing except the outside of a building, with a few women and one man going about their business beyond the big windows on which the name Delangle & Abouet was painted in gold letters.

"Anything new at the office?"

"Yes. Gisèle's beginning her vacation on August 15, too. They're going to Brittany, near Paimpol."

"Who'll take care of her brother's drawings?"

"I have no idea. Anyway, I'm not going to run around to the newspapers."

"Why don't they take him with them?"

"If you think they want to burden themselves with a cripple . . ."

Before their exchange of confidences, she wouldn't have blushed or tried to explain away her words. Now she was embarrassed, and gave him an almost suppliant look.

"I'm so sorry! What I mean is that Gisèle's a woman who expects everything from other people; she finds it natural they should take all kinds of trouble for her, but she herself wouldn't lift a finger for anybody."

"I understood."

"You're sure? I'm always so afraid of hurting your feel-ings! . . . Two of the bosses are away, at Evian—they have a house there. That leaves only old Monsieur Delangle."

Again she had avoided mentioning Jean-Paul by name. The other day she'd said emphatically that he took no interest in anything except business and modernizing the firm. Still, he had a powerful sports car. Did the two things go together?

"Aubonne hasn't come in?"

"Why should he? It's not time. . . ."

"No, of course not. When it gets toward August, with everybody on the move, it's hard to keep track. By the way, which shops are closing?"

"More than half of them in the first two weeks. The shoemaker's gone already, for three weeks. Guess where?"

"To the Riviera?"

"To Italy! The butcher's leaving on Monday with his family, and I'll have to go to rue du Pas-de-la-Mule to buy the meat. The dairy's closing only for a week, but it will close again when the wine harvest comes along, because they have a little vineyard on the Loire. . . ."

Those were the pleasantest moments. That kind of thing was definite and reassuring. It belonged to the impersonal life to which, involuntarily, they belonged. They had only to lean out the window to see people going about their business, looking cheerful or cross, buses following their appointed routes, taxis driving to the addresses they had been given.

Monsieur Jussieu had gone away for a month, and the click of his typewriter and the continual ringing of his telephone, which he answered in nasal tones and usually in a foreign language, could no longer be heard.

As for Monsieur and Madame Meilhan, the old couple

on the fourth floor, they were scarcely remembered; in the end, they would vanish discreetly, one after the other, like Monsieur François.

They, too, were shut up in a world of their own, where from time to time the old lady tried to make herself audible to her husband. From the street, his head could be seen behind the cast-iron arabesques of the window rail; he was capable of sitting for hours, motionless, doing nothing.

Was he thinking? Was he turning over memories of a time when he'd been a young man, full of activity, probably in love? Or was he saying to himself that one of these days the ray of sunshine that turned his white hair into a kind of halo would be shining on an empty chair?

Other Mazerons must already be watching that apartment. Perhaps the concierge had a list of names.

And suppose Bernard Foy was the first to go? Suppose that, contrary to what they had led him to believe, his dizziness was a symptom of dangerous illness?

If so, had his wife been warned? Did that account for her sweetness, her little attentions, her fear of crossing him in any way?

She never stayed more than a couple of minutes in Pierre Mazeron's apartment, and he'd noticed that when she went in she took care not to shut the door, leaving it just ajar. It wasn't that she pushed it that far; the door swung to of its own accord, like theirs, because the house was lopsided.

She no longer waited for him to question her.

"Gisèle's parents sent her a sausage, and she sent him a piece of it. . . ."

Bernard had tried to get a glimpse of the young man. He was still trying, doing his best to get back from his shopping just when the nurse arrived, to be on the landing when she opened the door. It was a silly game, but he played it every morning. What made his success unlikely was that the nurse arrived on a motorbike. She left it by the curb, and, being young and nimble, she was up on the second floor in a flash.

He couldn't wait on the stairs for her. And it was too late to go back on his decision not to take in the package or letter instead of Nelly.

"It seems to me you've been better these last few days. . . ."

She was deceived. He was hiding his thoughts more carefully, that was all; and of course she didn't see him when he was alone.

When she was there, he forced himself to seem content, carefree. He took her out for the Grand Tour, and she had no suspicion that for him it was a kind of pilgrimage. He watched the Seine flow by as he'd watched it so many times; then he gazed at the buildings one by one, as though all this already belonged to the past. He looked for the white-haired old gentleman in his red leather armchair, but the shutters of the splendid library were closed. Nearly every-body was away.

"I love you, Nelly."

"And I love you, Bernard."

"I want you to know it really, to feel it."

"I do know it. I do feel it."

He was on the point of adding: "It's because I love you that I'm making us both unhappy."

But what would be the good? He was no longer even sure if it was true!

Chapter Seven

H E HAD MANAGED it at last, by accident, one day when he wasn't even trying. He was coming home from shopping—he'd had to go to rue Saint-Antoine, because most of the shops on their street were shut. He had bought enough potatoes for several days, and in addition to the meat and groceries, he was bringing back a fine melon and some apricots that had tempted him on a street cart.

The net bag was dangling heavily from his hook, and he had paused for breath in the shadowy hallway. The concierge was not in her lodge. He had just set foot on the bottom step when he heard the motorbike stop outside.

He began to walk up slowly, so the nurse would have to go past him. Her rapid steps were approaching. Then she slipped by between him and the wall. When she reached the landing, he was three steps below, just as he had planned.

He was almost sure she'd never noticed him, because he

had always seen her from behind or in three-quarter profile, and she was always in a hurry, paying no attention to what was happening around her.

Yet before putting her hand on the doorknob she looked around—not to stare at his books, like someone seeing him for the first time, not with surprise or curiosity, but with the air of knowing who he was.

Had Mazeron told her about him? At any rate, she treated him like a neighbor, pointing to his bag with the remark "That looks heavy. You wouldn't like me to help you?"

"I'm used to it. Thank you . . ."

She did not insist, merely adding with a smile: "You've got a fine melon."

He was right in the middle of the landing, still looking in her direction, when she opened the door. So at last he saw. Not for long. Not everything. But enough to give him a surprise.

Because Monsieur François was a very old man and had lived for years like a recluse, and because that door was an ugly drab color, Bernard had taken it for granted that the apartment, which overlooked the courtyard, was dark and gloomy. The concierge did the housework, but was none too thorough. One might even say she was a slut.

But at the far end of a narrow hall, he had seen bright yellow walls, which gave the room a light, cheerful appearance.

He had had time to notice a very long white wood table—on trestles—covered with all kinds of objects. There were pencils standing point upward in a small blue earthenware pot; there were sticks of charcoal in another pot; there were paintbrushes, scattered papers, magazines, and newspapers, a vase of flowers, half a croissant lying beside a cup. . . .

It gave him the impression that, unlike any other apartment—their own, for instance—it was a place where things did not have any fixed position, where life could run on as it chose.

He had not been able to see the nudes, and all he had seen of Mazeron was his legs and one rubber-tired wheel of his chair.

It was cheerful! The most cheerful apartment in the house, surely. It must be a nice place to live, amid that picturesque disorder, which would give life an effervescent quality. The artist must be cheerful, too. It was undoubtedly he, not Monsieur François, who had chosen that exultant yellow for the walls and that shade of red for the curtains, seen from outside.

When he went back into their own apartment, it seemed to him, by comparison, heavy and dull, conventional—in his own image, no doubt, since it was he who had arranged it. Didn't he sometimes get up from his chair to replace a copper pot in its exact position, straighten a fold in the curtain, or put a newspaper neatly away on the shelf under the radio?

Though he was not surprised by his discovery, it left its mark on him. He had indeed imagined Mazeron to be young, easygoing, but even so he thought of him differently after that peep into his apartment.

The nurse had apparently known who he was. So she knew there was a man without hands living there. And since Mazeron had never seen him, it must have come through Nelly.

Nelly talked about him on the second floor. Then the young man, in his turn . . .

At lunchtime he didn't mention what had happened on the landing, but he could not resist bringing Mazeron into the conversation.

"How does he sign his drawings?"

The name was seldom or never mentioned. It was always "he," but both of them realized who was meant. True, they knew few people and seldom referred to anybody in conversation.

She frowned, as though searching her memory. If she was putting on an act, it was done to perfection.

"Gisèle told me once. . . . Wait a minute. . . ."

That showed that Gisèle and she talked about him, not only in connection with errands. The way Mazeron signed his drawings had nothing to do with the fact of taking him a letter or a package. Maybe it was he, not his sister, who'd told her.

"He uses two syllables of his name. . . . I've got it! He signs 'Mapi,' the first syllable of his surname and the first two letters of his Christian name."

"Have you seen his stuff?"

"Gisèle showed me one of his little drawings. . . ."

She seemed quite at ease. But she couldn't be, in reality. That was what made the situation rather hopeless. If there was anything between her and Gisèle's brother, if she had had a relationship with any man at all, she was bound to hide it from him at all costs, if only from charity.

She couldn't suddenly admit: "You're right to be jealous. I'm like the others, like your Alsatian woman; but I love you all the same and I want to stay with you."

He would have kept her, of course. He wouldn't have reproached her. On the contrary, he would no doubt have been even more affectionate and considerate, knowing that she was unhappy.

He had been sincere, when they lay side by side on the bed, staring up at the ceiling. Had he really told everything? Weren't there some shameful little patches he preferred to overlook and hadn't spoken of?

On the other hand, even if Nelly did care nothing for Mazeron and that, as she maintained, she never could have gone to bed with another man than Bernard, or even contemplated such a thing, the fact remained that she knew he was scrutinizing her reactions, that he was on the watch for a glance, a facial expression, or even a slight start, from which he would draw God knows what dramatic conclusions.

So there again, how could she be natural?

And yet she was—too much so. It made him furious to feel that Mazeron was always between them, invisibly, even at their quiet meals; and it was he who couldn't help bringing the man into the conversation!

He so much longed to know exactly what lay behind his wife's brow, at the back of her eyes. Ten times a day he would ask her, point-blank: "What are you thinking about?"

Sometimes her reply would be unexpected.

"About your sister."

"Why are you thinking about her?"

"Because your mother hasn't written to us for quite a long time. I was saying to myself that we'd go see her during my vacation, and I was wondering whether your sister had got any fatter. . . ."

Last time they had visited Juvisy, taking a present for each of the children and a big tart for the whole family, his sister had been enormous, and it looked as if she'd get still fatter. She was delighted about it, and moved briskly in spite of her big body. Moreover, she was the first to laugh at herself.

Nelly had not thought up that idea to meet the occasion, so there must, inevitably, be other thoughts she was hiding from him. If Aubonne was anxious about him, for instance, she, as his wife, must be even more worried. But she never spoke to him about it. One doesn't speak to a man about his illness if he doesn't think he is ill.

Since she was capable of keeping things back from him on that subject, why shouldn't she be concealing other matters?

He could scarcely see into his own mind, so how could he expect to read hers?

Instead of perpetually repeating words that had no meaning, what they needed was to find some way of looking at each other that would make everything clear.

He had sometimes thought that must be possible. He would look into her eyes, moved and anxious, and say softly: "I love you, Nelly!"

It was rather like a key. He waited for the response. It seemed to him that there was always a kind of sadness at the back of his wife's eyes as she answered, meeting his gaze: "And I love you, Bernard."

Why the sadness? Because she felt guilty and self-reproachful, or because he was tormenting himself for no reason and she couldn't prevent this, for all her love—because she couldn't manage to make him happy?

"What color is his bedroom?"

"His bedroom?" she repeated, not understanding for a second. Then she went on: "I've never seen his bedroom; only the studio. That's painted yellow, like the hall."

"What newspapers does he work for?"

"I suppose he sends things wherever he can, like all beginners. Which is the paper that has its offices on rue Montmartre?"

"How should I know?"

"Rue Montmartre is where Gisèle goes most often."

He had been able to answer her question the very next day, because he had bought all the weekly papers that published cartoons and found three signed "Mapi." That evening he showed them to Nelly.

"Look."

"Where?"

"At the bottom of the page, on the left . . ."

She laughed. The caption was funny.

"You say he works at night?" he asked again.

"Presumably. Because he always asks me to drop in in the morning to see if he's been able to get anything done."

"And during the day?"

"I don't know how he spends his time."

She didn't venture to add: "Do stop talking about him every day, at every meal! It's becoming an obsession. You're making yourself ill."

He told himself so, tried to think of other things. He went to the public library, where he hadn't set foot for a long time, and took out two novels. He began one of them, but he couldn't concentrate.

To make matters worse, the increasing emptiness of his surroundings added to his feeling of solitude. There wasn't a sound from the Rougins' apartment since the twins had gone away with their parents. Mademoiselle Strieb was away, too. There were fewer trucks, cars, and buses passing along the street, and he sometimes caught himself wondering at the silence as though it were abnormal.

Outdoors he no longer met familiar faces, only foreigners in gaudy shirts, carrying cameras; sometimes they crept stealthily into the alleyway for an inquisitive stare around the courtyard.

Another five—four—three days, and Nelly, too, would be on vacation. He would have her to himself from morning till night, from night till morning, and he wouldn't need to ask himself what she was doing, to whom she was talking, whose voice she was listening to.

He was reveling in the idea, as he did every year, though he was a little anxious at the thought of three weeks' uninterrupted tête-à-tête.

Would he manage to talk naturally to her? Would he find enough inoffensive subjects of conversation? In the old days he hadn't worried, had talked of anything or nothing; often they had both fallen silent without noticing it.

Nowadays he was afraid of silence. It gave him the impression he could feel Nelly thinking, behind the barrier of her forehead, and he set traps for her, tried to think of questions that might cut the ground from under her feet.

If this continued, he ought to call Aubonne and ask him to come, or go and see him. He should force himself to tell the doctor everything and, above all, ask definite questions, beg him to answer them frankly, not so much for his own sake as for his wife's.

Was he really ill? That was surely the first point to clear up. Neither Pellet nor Aubonne had ever been precise about that long-standing fracture of the petrosal bone. When he had asked whether it might still cause trouble, they didn't say yes or no; they seemed embarrassed.

"In some cases . . ."

What kind of trouble, exactly? That was the second question. For instance, might it affect his spirits? It was most unlikely that his problem was unique. Aubonne must have come across others. His patients included not only ex-servicemen, but also men suffering from industrial injuries. That was his specialty. He didn't try to find wealthy patients. He lived just off the Faubourg Saint-Antoine, among the craftsmen and skilled workers on rue Crozatier, opposite the hospital; and although his apartment was spacious and comfortably furnished, the working-class people in his district didn't feel out of place in it.

But jealousy was not an illness doctors could cure. He must heal himself, or get used to living with it, as he had for twenty years, when it made him suffer only now and then, and not so violently.

"I'm sure she's tormenting herself," he sometimes said in an undertone when he was alone.

He would talk to her as he went from the bedroom to the living room and the living room to the kitchen, as though she were there.

"You see, it's beyond my control. . . . I'm not responsible for it. . . . I'm doing my best. . . . Maybe it's because I blame myself. . . .

"At a certain age, the age I'm getting to now, one tries to take stock of one's past life, as though that might give one courage to go on. . . . And when I began to take stock, I realized I'd always been selfish.

"I wanted to shut myself up in an apartment, with only its windows opening to the world outside; and I shut you up with me. . . ."

His one sacrifice—and even that he had made only on Aubonne's advice—had been to allow Nelly to keep her job outside. Hadn't he been prompted by an ulterior motive? Hadn't he said to himself that if she stayed with him all day, shut up on rue de Turenne, they would become peevish, testy?

He let her go to Place des Victoires, but calculated the exact time she needed to get there and back. On the rare occasions when she had shopping to do in town, he went with her and waited outside for her, even if she was buying lingerie. If he did allow her to go by herself, he questioned her endlessly about what she had done, what people had said to her, whom she had met.

"Tell me, doctor . . ."

Had Nelly and Aubonne talked about him when he wasn't there? Very likely, at least in the beginning. The doctor must have explained her husband's condition to her, reassured her, and given her advice. Had he told her to be careful, to protect him from any kind of worry?

"I love you, Nelly!"

"And I love you, Bernard."

They were saying this much more often than they used to, as though trying to kindle a spark. Sometimes he had the feeling that they had succeeded, that he was suddenly released, that life was about to begin again in the old way. He forgot Mazeron, the door with the ivory-white china knob, the yellow-painted studio with the cluttered table.

"You know what we'll do, after we've been to see Mother and my sister?"

"You have a plan?"

The faintest ray of hope transformed her, and then he would feel she was really happy, not just pretending.

"We'll choose a different part of Paris every day, like we used to do on Sundays when we first came to live here—in the days when, once we were on the Grands Boulevards, we never knew which direction the Etoile was in and which the Bastille. . . . We'll start early. . . ."

He had always loved the streets early in the morning.

"We'll stroll around like tourists, wander into court-yards, and every day at lunchtime we'll choose some quaint little restaurant. . . ."

"You feel better, don't you, Bernard?"

"Did I worry you a lot?"

"Not too much. I had confidence."

"You know, I wonder whether I was right to talk to you the way I did. I wanted to be honest, no matter what it cost. It brought to the surface a whole pack of ideas, the kind everyone has, I suppose, in some corner of their minds, the kind it's best not to take seriously. . . . The fact is, I was missing you. . . . I needed you, and our vacation time. . . ."

"You haven't had any more dizzy spells?"

"Not many."

This was not true. He'd had one that very morning; but he wanted to cheer her up. As to the rest, he was quite sincere.

"I'm just an old fool who doesn't deserve a wife like you. If you knew what suspicions I've had about you!"

"Don't talk about it any more. Don't think about it any more!"

"You're not angry with me?"

"How could I be? It must be my fault entirely. If I'd managed to make you understand . . ."

Of course! That was the whole problem! To strip naked in front of each other. Not their bodies—their minds. All the little thoughts that go around in one's head and belong only to oneself.

"If that imitation bistro in the Latin Quarter is still there, we could . . ."

He would no longer be alarmed by the prices on the menu, or have to find an excuse for leaving.

"Did you ask Gisèle how he'll manage about his drawings during her vacation?"

"I suppose the nurse will take care of them."

"Isn't she going away?"

"Not until September, when a friend who'll take her place gets back."

"You still don't know if it's she who sat for the nudes?"

"No. I only pop in and out. I must admit it doesn't interest me."

When he was at his most jealous, it excited him to think of the nurse, naked and motionless, in the yellow studio. He envied Mazeron. He envied his job, which seemed to him like a perpetual game, his youth, his lightheartedness. And now, on top of all that, he was envying him his nurse!

He didn't tell Nelly that. So he was cheating! Didn't that give her the right to cheat in return?

Another three days, another two days . . .

Chapter Eight

IT WAS THURSDAY MORNING, and a sunny day again, with a slight breeze down in the streets, along which water wagons were passing slowly. Nelly was off to Place des Victoires. She would go there again tomorrow, and then, on Saturday, she'd be on vacation and could stay in bed late.

She had given Bernard his bath and helped him on with his prosthesis. One of these days they would go, as they did periodically, to have it overhauled by old Hélias, on rue du Chemin-Vert. There had been one croissant left on the plate at breakfast.

"Aren't you going to eat it?" Nelly had asked.

"No."

"Then I will. It's my fourth!"

He had watched her while he smoked his first cigarette. She was wearing a light-colored linen suit, and her breasts looked younger and more alive under the blouse than under a dress. He noticed that when they quivered they seemed to have a life of their own, and that excited him.

He didn't say "I love you."

He smiled at her, feeling relaxed, thinking he would go out and do the shopping on rue Saint-Antoine, where childhood memories greeted him at every step.

He liked the little carts along the sidewalks, the cries of the women, the shops that opened right onto the street, the day's bargains chalked up on slates.

"Tomorrow evening . . ." he said softly.

She stood up, straightened her skirt, and planted herself in front of him to give him a kiss.

"We'll have lots of fun; you'll see. . . ."

"I always have fun with you!"

On her way out she added: "I've put lipstick on your cheek. . . ."

He heard her go downstairs. In a moment he would go to the window to wave to her. He wondered whether to clear the table before going out to do the shopping. But feeling in a hurry to get out of doors, into the sparkling morning, he decided to do it when he got back.

He was listening, as usual. She'd stopped on the second floor, which was not unusual. It suddenly occurred to him that he could collect his net bag and hurry down, to surprise her by reaching the foot of the stairs at almost the same time she did.

It was all quite fortuitous. He had no ulterior motive. He had waked up in a cheerful mood and was still in one.

He went down without touching the railing with his hook, which was a good sign. He moved quickly, eager to be in time to say good-bye to her again.

He felt a little uneasy, though, at not hearing her come out of the second-floor apartment. Maybe she'd only looked in for an instant, and was outside already. Maybe,

132

for once, Mazeron had been waiting for her just inside the door and had simply given her his drawings as she went by, if he had any to give her.

He reached the third floor and, once past the bend, saw that the door on the next floor was ajar. At this, the bright mood deserted him. He frowned, calculating that his wife had been in there for nearly five minutes.

On the landing he hesitated, pausing to give her another chance. At the same time, he told himself he was making a mistake, that he would embarrass her, that when she came out and ran into him they wouldn't know what to say to each other. And the whole thing would begin all over again.

Why did he suddenly take a step forward and push the door open? He did it almost unconsciously, obeying an instinctive, irresistible impulse.

Just as on the morning when the nurse had gone in while he stood there, he saw the long hall, the brighter light in the yellow studio; and, beside the trestle table with its load of drawings and magazines, Nelly, her back to him, bending over a seated man, who held her clasped in his arms.

Without seeing their faces, he realized that their mouths were pressed together, that his wife was trying to free herself—no doubt because she had heard the sound of the door—and that she was about to look around.

He retreated at once, almost closing the door behind him, rushed downstairs, and dashed out to the street without pausing at the lodge, though the concierge was waving an envelope at him.

He was so stupefied that he did not apologize when he ran headlong into an elderly woman and sent her packages flying. He didn't pick them up; while she grumbled and gesticulated, he went on his way, his knees shaking and his mind a blank.

He wasn't thinking—any more than when his hands had touched the mine and he had become the center of an explosion. He followed his normal route to rue Saint-Antoine. He passed, unheeding, by the house where he had been born, and turned into rue de Birague without recognizing it.

He was not questioning himself, not asking himself what would happen now, or what he was going to do. For months he had been thinking about it, tormenting himself, as though deliberately, with detailed pictures, compared with which the one he had just seen was comparatively innocuous.

In fact, he'd foreseen everything. Perhaps it was he who had tripped some kind of mechanism.

He had no further need to try to find out. He knew, now. He didn't blame Nelly. He had always declared that he wouldn't.

He wondered whether to run back to rue de Turenne. But he wasn't sure if she had seen him. She had heard the faint creak of the door, but that might have been caused by a draft. While she was releasing herself from Mazeron's arms, and was about to look around, he was retreating. It had been a matter of seconds, of a fraction of a second. Had she had time to catch sight of his back, his shoulders, before the door swung to?

The woman who'd sold him the melon had a fresh load of them. She tried to attract his attention, and he yielded. She chose one for him and put it into his bag. For the first time, he fumbled in taking the money out of his purse, as though his hooks had suddenly acquired the faculty of trembling, like hands. It was so visible that the woman was startled and asked, "What's the matter with you, dearie?"

"Nothing . . ."

His throat was dry, as he discovered when he tried to speak. He forced himself to smile politely, as one does at strangers who have done you no harm. He could feel she was looking after him and shaking her head, and knew she felt sorry for him without knowing why. He remembered what he had to buy. He needed ham and salad, since they had decided on a cold lunch. He went to the Italian shop.

He stopped twice on the way, in the crowd, beside a wall, so he could lean against it if necessary; he was afraid of falling over. He knew he wouldn't really fall, that it was not serious, only a little alarming.

"It's my own fault. . . ."

He spoke aloud, as he had got into the habit of doing lately when he was alone in the apartment.

"It was bound to happen. . . ."

There! There was nothing more to be said. It had happened!

He'd better do the shopping just the same. Nelly would be back at twenty past twelve, as usual, and they'd have to have lunch.

"Four slices of ham on the bone . . ."

He looked, without really seeing them, at the dishes displaying a variety of vegetable salads, and pointed with his hook at two of them.

"Half a pound of each of those."

They knew him here. They asked how he was, how his wife was, and he replied politely.

"She's very well."

"When are you going on vacation?"

"The day after tomorrow."

They didn't follow this up by asking where; to which he could only have replied, "Nowhere."

He was nowhere, really. The world was still around him, but more unreal than at his very worst moments. Sounds were muffled to his ears, as though Pellet had been right in declaring that he was growing deaf.

"Shall I put these on your account?"

"Yes, please."

They had accounts at several shops. They really belonged to the district.

He almost forgot they needed butter; he went into the first dairy he came to, the one on rue de Turenne being closed.

"A pound of Brittany butter."

There was hardly any waiting. Customers were much fewer at this time of year. As he went back along rue de Birague, he saw only a dog on the sidewalk, lying with its paws in the air and rolling slowly to scratch its back.

"A letter for you!" called the concierge.

He took it absentmindedly and put it in his pocket, while she watched him with the same look on her face as the melon woman had had.

Reaching their floor, he realized with surprise that he had not slowed down on the second, or even glanced at the door with the china knob. His obsession seemed to have left him at last.

"I'll tell her. . . ."

He didn't know what, exactly. He would say simple, affectionate, consoling things, as though to a sick person— the kind of things she often said to him, looking at him with her limpid, tranquil eyes.

He was not being ironical. He was genuinely remembering his wife's tranquil, innocent eyes, and he did not want any change to come to them.

He would tell her. . . . He felt in his pocket for the key, and noticed that the door was not locked. Either he had forgotten to do it when he went out, which seldom happened, or else Nelly had come up again, perhaps thinking he had returned to the apartment.

The living room was just as he had left it. A little coffee remained in his wife's cup; none in his own, since he always drained it to the last drop. He carried his purchases through to the kitchen, opened the refrigerator, and put in the butter, ham, and salads.

He did it all mechanically. It had not occurred to him to weep, rebel, or feel sorry for himself. The fog had cleared, and everything had become simple, with the harsh distinctness of certain photographs.

What had he forgotten? Nothing. Oh, yes—the window overlooking rue des Minimes was shut, and he went to open it, because they always liked it open in hot weather. The bedroom door was closed. That surprised him. He was almost sure it had been open when he left.

He opened it automatically, and saw Nelly lying on her back, fully dressed, in her place on the far side of the bed. She was looking up at the ceiling, like she had that afternoon they had made love, slowly, each of them trying to pass completely into the other.

He had intended to speak to her, so he did.

"I thought . . ."

As he went around the bed, he saw his wife's arm hanging down above the rug. A pool of blood had formed. Blood had splashed on the wall, and one of the kitchen knives, the one he'd recently had sharpened, lay on the floor.

He went to her and bent down. Taking her head in his hands, slowly and gently, as though afraid of hurting her or waking her, he pressed his mouth against hers and remained like that for a long time, with closed eyes.

He knew she was dead. He had known it at once. He

closed her eyes, still moving cautiously. Then he lifted the arm with the wide gash on the wrist, and laid it on the bed.

He was through with questions, once and for all. He had all the answers, and he looked at the void that surrounded him. His eye was caught by a piece of paper lying on his pillow.

"Forgive me," she had written.

Nothing else. There was nothing else to be said.

"Forgive me . . ."

He stammered the words, adding very softly: "I love you, Nelly. . . ."

No voice could answer now: "And I love you, Bernard."

Why did he go to make sure that the gas was properly turned off, as he used to when they were going out together? Then he went into the bathroom, where there was a medicine cabinet with all the drugs prescribed to help him sleep.

He took ten pills of one kind and ten of another, choosing the strongest; then he filled a glass with water and swallowed them, one by one. Walking back through the living room, he looked at the table, Nelly's place, her cup— and he drank the dregs of cold coffee left in it, to drive away the taste of the pills.

He was calm, not sad. Since his wife had kept on her light-colored suit, he kept his clothes on when he lay down beside her, on his back, as he had the other day. He waited, looking up at the ceiling and talking to her, very softly, telling her all the sweet, trifling things he had never been able to put into words.